TALL W
consp

by

Michael Ellis

Based on the screenplay by
Tony O'Leary and Michael Ellis

Tallwhites.org

MAMBI BOOKS

First published in Great Britain by Mambi Books, 2017

The Studio, High Green, Great Shelford, Cambridge CB22 5EG

Copyright © 2017 Kimura International Development Limited.

ISBN: 978-1-903500-53-8

All rights reserved, including the right to reproduce this book, or portions thereof in any form. No part of this text may be reproduced, transmitted, downloaded, decompiled, reverse engineered or stored, in any form, or introduced into any information storage and retrieval system, in any form or by any means, whether electronic or mechanical without the express written permission of the author(s).

PROLOG

Transcript.
'From Our Own Correspondent'.
BBC Radio 4.
First broadcast March 27.
No longer available for download.

Coral Donovan: Meanwhile, we are in New York, at the United Nations, where climate scientists, aviation experts and world leaders gathered this week to find a solution to the global air emergency and hopefully, a way to end the worldwide ban on flying. Even amid the week's tragedies and the mayhem in world markets, events there have taken a bizarre turn, as our correspondent Nick Hare reports:

Nick Hare: New York is cold in March, very cold, and smoking has been banned indoors since 2003. One place that was free of the ban was the International Zone, that part of the Big Apple that is outside the U.S. and beyond state or city jurisdiction. The United Nations, created to bring the people of the world together, took another five years to force smokers into external exile. And while smoking is banned in public parks in New York you will still find a handful of dedicated smokers on the sidewalks near the General Assembly building on even the coldest days.

But today was different. Today, hundreds of people flooded out on to United Nations Plaza and East 44th. People from every part of the planet, of every persuasion and race and gender, and all in a state of agitation, in some cases, of exhilaration but mostly plain old panic.

Aside from United Nations staff and security officials, they were experts drawn from every sphere and every institution that could reach this location without using air travel. They were called here in a completely unprecedented move, within hours of events the world has yet to comprehend. Even to take in. They were here to find out why eight planes, civilian passenger jets, military and cargo aircraft crashed in a single day in a single area being called the Nevada Triangle.

As the death toll rises, debris is scattered over thousands of square miles of the western United States. A state of emergency declared throughout the West, Nevada and New Mexico; all flights over the continental U.S.A. grounded; the worst aviation disaster in history. Its cause: still a mystery

These men and women were – are – here to find out why it happened and how to prevent a second such catastrophe, and when, if ever, it will be safe to fly again. Short of stopping a war or an epidemic, it is perhaps the most serious challenge imaginable. It is mirrored by the efforts of tens of thousands of men and women from the services, government agencies, from Park Rangers to fire fighters, the National Guard and volunteers grimly searching the crash sites for clues.

But, oddly, that was not the cause of this morning's panic at the United Nations. No. It was the appearance of an alien. A man from outer space. That's right. E.T. Mister Spock. An extraterrestrial.

Perhaps it is a measure of the febrile atmosphere within this building that so many rational and dedicated, intelligent individuals could be spooked into a stampede.

At 10.08 precisely, in that building, a man, yet to be identified, joined the General Secretary of the United Nations on the rostrum. So far, so ordinary. What happened next defies explanation.

According to witness after witness the man addressed the assembled experts – apparently in their own languages and without the need for the army of simultaneous translators who normally assist these meetings.

And (I quote directly from Professor Mary Craig-Pedersen, the Chief Scientist of the United Nations Environment Program), 'he told us we face an extinction event. The end of humanity. Of life on Earth. He told us it is being brought about by aliens and our own people. He said he was an alien. An actual alien. And then he combusted. He vanished in a bright light, like an angel, and we ran.'

Alien, angel or illusion, what is most extraordinary about this account is that it is repeated by almost everyone who was there. They are engineers, climate scientists, aviation experts. Even reporters. They all say the same. A man, to all appearances like the rest of us, spoke in tongues. He declared himself to be from the other side of the Universe. He delivered an apocalyptic warning. And then transformed into a beam of incorporeal light.

New York City Police Commissioner Alvin Chappi blames a mass hallucination. As he puts it: 'We are all scared, at this time. You have got to expect some craziness.'

The Department of Homeland Security has categorically denied that anything happened at all.

So far, there is no clue to the identity, motivation or fate of the so-called alien. Nor any hard proof of his existence. U.N. security guards have refused to release video of what happened.

The alleged event sparked a Twitterstorm among U.F.O. conspiracy theorists who link the catastrophic cluster of airplane crashes to the existence of a race of space aliens they call the Tall Whites. As evidence, they point out that the mysterious and tragic crashes occurred within an 800 mile radius of Las Vegas, which as some listeners will know, is close to Area 51, a notorious flying saucer 'hot spot' since shortly after World War Two.

Conspiracy theorists are renowned for making connections where none exist, of seeing patterns where there are none. This conspiracy theory goes further than most. It says aliens have been running a parallel government in the U.S.A. for more than half a century – after President Dwight D. Eisenhower struck a deal with creatures from outer space, for advanced technology.

Quite what Ike gave for it or got from it, they don't say. But the self-styled 'ufologists' claim it was the worst deal since the one struck in 1609 by Seyseys, the Native American chief who sold Manhattan – the island on which the United Nations building stands today – to the Dutchman Peter Minuit, for just sixty guilders, or about twenty-four dollars.

If the U.N. alien is a hoax – and I would bet my last sixty Guilders that it is – it is a cruel one and a distraction at a time of tragedy and danger. In the cosmically, mind-bogglingly, unlikely event that an alien being has delivered such a warning, and that it is true, the calamity that struck in the Nevada Triangle could be just the start, with worse, possibly far worse, to come.

My sixty guilders says that is not the case. But the fact is, the world changed this week and we can take nothing for granted, other than, as Police Commissioner Chappi put it, 'we are all scared, at this time. You have got to expect some craziness.'

This is Nick Hare, B.B.C. New York.

Chapter One

Question One

'Do you know why you're here?'

'What is this? A philosophy class?'

If the military-looking man sees the joke, it doesn't register.

'Do you know why you're here? 'The voice: flat.

'Where is "here"?'

This guy; this military-looking guy. Something about him. Familiar but not familiar. He's a type. Bullet-head. Flat-top. Stocky. Clean-shaven. Too clean-shaven. Maybe some Hispanic in there. Or Italian. No glasses. No watch visible. Clean shirt, long-sleeved, pressed. No necktie. The room: wood table (new), utility chairs with canvas backs, metals frames: two. Walls: Cray, painted cinder block. Floor, ceiling: concrete, also painted. One light. Metal coolie shade. Dark green outside. White inside. But the light: diffuse, cold, like light from a tube. And the door? No door behind the military guy. None visible to the left or right. Keep eye contact.

'You don't know?'

'Whatever you want from me I haven't got it. Whatever you want to know, I don't know it.'

'Why don't you tell me something? Like who you are. Or get out of my face?'

'Who I am, Dave?'

Peripheral vision sucks. There must be a door. No draft. No presence. But it must be there. Locked? Open? What does he want? Wait. Wait. Did he call me Dave?

'You haven't even got the right guy. I'm not Dave anything. I'm Michael Roland. '

'Good. Michael.'

'I am Michael Roland. Michael Raymond Roland. U.S. citizen. Non-criminal. Non-terrorist. Non-Dave. If you think you've got Dave, you've got the wrong guy.'

'What do you do for a living, Michael?'

'I'm a teacher. I teach.'

'At Boston U.'

'At Boston U. You clearly know that already. What is this?'

'Why are you here?'

'I shouldn't be here.'

'Where do you want to be?'

'Out of here. Wherever this is. Home.'

No movement of the hands. No movement, period. No expression. What the hell has happened? I feel so tired. So tired.

'You can't keep me here. I haven't done anything.'

'That's not strictly correct, Mike.'

What is not correct? That I can't go or I did something? Nothing. Say something, you bastard.

'Are you for real?'

'Yes.'

'Do I know you?'

'Don't you?'

'No.'

'That's a pity. We have a problem.'

'What problem?'

'A big problem.'

Chapter Two

The sword of Damocles

Washington D.C., Summer, 1952

Secret Service agent Floyd M. Boring was instantly conscious of the weight of the .38-caliber Detective Special on his right hip. The sensation accompanied an instinctive adjustment of his bulk, a slight turn of the stocky body to present a narrower target and make the gun quicker to draw. Then he recognized the walk, loping and long-paced, as press secretary Joseph Short lolloped along the corridor like a pallid gun dog cradling a still-warm duck in its jaws. A squarer figure with a brisker stride was moving up fast on the inside, solid-framed, with crinkly silver hair and heavy black eyebrows over a pair of steel blue eyes. Air Force General Nathan Farragut Twining never had time to waste. Tonight was no exception.

'The President is sleeping, sir,' said Boring.

'He never sleeps,' barked Twining as he moved into the space between Short and the guard.

'Sir. It is close on midnight and the President is…'

'I am aware… We are aware of the President's condition but we must talk with him,' said the more emollient Short as Twining moved into the space between him and the guard.

'This is national security,' snapped the general. Short nodded.

'Stay here, sir,' Boring said, holding out his gun hand to indicate an imaginary deadline. He opened the door into the President's apartments far enough to enter while completely filling the temporary gap.

Within a minute, Boring re-emerged ahead of Wallace Graham. 'Harry's breathing is like bees in a paper sack,' rasped the physician. 'The man's never been ill in his life before. Nothing like this. This had better be urgent.'

'Have you looked out of the window?' Twining demanded.

'Can't say I have, General. I am not disposed to taking in the view when I have a 68-year-old patient with a temperature of 106 in my charge.'

'You had better look out there now.'

Graham had taken bullets in both legs and his left hand at different times on the ground in Europe. He had had his share of excitement, which is why is he hadn't minded becoming 'the most disemployed doctor' in the history of medicine, tending to the Trumans. But Harry S. Truman's pneumonia had hit both of them hard. Truman was, in fact, recovering, but Harry was the most powerful man in the world and Graham wasn't about to go down in history as the quack that killed him. Boring noticed how worn Graham was after a week with as near as dammit no sleep; how he hauled himself around as if he had a corpse clinging to each limb. But as Graham reached the tall sash window his posture changed. Rigid, Graham could see a huge light, or maybe a shining silvery disk, hovering in the late evening sky. He peered, trying to make sense of what he saw. 'What the hell is it? It's too bright for anything like a balloon and it sure as heck ain't a cloud. Is it some sort of stunt? A trick?'

'They're real enough,' said Twining. 'And there's more of them. One in each quadrant.'

'Some kind of helicopter?'

'No noise. No draft.'

'Are they dangerous?'

'They haven't shown themselves to be but we sent up an L15 scout and before the pilot could get anywhere close his engine stalled. He glided away. The engine picked up. He flew back. It stalled again.'

'Dammed if they don't look like foo fighters,' said Graham.

'We can't say that,' said Short.

'I saw one of those trailing us on a night mission over Germany in forty-four,' Graham mused. 'The difference was they moved like stink; they weren't static like these guys. They flitted around, banked, maneuvered, sped up. There was no way we could even catch up with them. Those Kraut fireballs were like sprites. But they were harmless. They just played with us.'

'They have been appearing for about a week outside Washington,' said Twining.

'That's about when Harry fell ill,' Graham interrupted. 'Damn. I had no idea.'

'... but these sons of bitches are in a pattern with the White House dead center,' said Twining. 'We have to assume they are making some kind of show. The President must be made aware. We may have to move him.'

Graham scowled. Twining led the way to the President's room as Boring took up position again by the door. He could just about make out one of the flying disks from where he stood. 'You think it's the Russians?' he heard Graham ask. 'I sure hope not,' Boring whispered to himself.

At Washington National Airport, Lane Kravitz could see the four objects in neat formation around the White House, holding their place at 2000 feet, the pips flashing at each sweep of the radar, so static he was tempted to scrape the thick glass of the scope. 'Have you got them?' he asked, instinctively cupping his hand over the mouthpiece of the phone.

'Yes I have them. Crazy thing is they ain't moving,' said Zacko from the airport's other center.

Senior air traffic controller Harry Barnes had seen systems affected by what the British called gremlins, before. 'If you can't see it with your own eyes you can't trust it, and you can't trust even if you can see it,' was his motto. 'You two guys check Kravitz's scope and then check it again,' he told McKenzie and Hare, just as his telephone rang. No guessing who. It was a direct line to Andrews Air Force Base, 10 miles away.

'Barnes. National.'

'Seven objects, fifteen, that's one-five miles Southwest quadrant. You got them?' demanded a voice from Andrews. 'Do you have anything in that area?'

'No known aircraft. That's not a flight path.'

'We have them traveling at one hundred to one three zero miles per hour. Can you check that?'

'Cocklin. Do you have seven objects on the scope? Fifteen miles out. Southwest quadrant.'

'Check'.

'What speed do you have?'

'Real slow. One hundred miles an hour. One twenty.'

'Zacko from Tower Two has One Twenty,' said Kravitz.

'Hey! That's weird!' shouted Hare. 'This pip just changed course by ninety degrees.'

'Check it again. That is impossible – for any plane,' shouted Barnes.

'Seven objects moving in a very, a very radical way. They keep changing direction but they're generally heading towards the Capitol… to where the static objects are,' Kravitz called. 'Holy cow. One has just stopped dead.'

'Check the scope,' snapped Barnes.

'Now they are really moving. Every sweep they are moving. They must be doing some incredible speed,' called Hare as he leaned over the wide, flat circle of scope, the lavender light pulsing slowly over his features every ten seconds with each sweep of the radar.

McKenzie hurriedly worked his slide rule. 'That is impossible,' he moaned.

'But the blips over the White House have not moved,' choked Kravitz, almost out of breath. 'Not an inch.'

'I can see them,' said the voice from the other tower. 'They are really erratic. I have them going off-course at ninety degrees then coming back again, then off again.'

'I've got them. I can see them,' said Barnes, peering through a pair of field glasses. 'I have a visual on one. It's a bright orange light. No. Red. Orange. I can't make out the shape. You got a velocity and altitude on that Kravitz?'

'Tracking rapid changes of direction and height,' spluttered Kravitz.

'Close to four thousand miles an hour at peak,' shouted McKenzie. 'They're just leaving dots across the scopes. Not just the main scope, the long range scopes too.'

'Zacko has them on the A.S.R. heading north-northeast toward Riverdale,' Kravitz called.

'Four thousand?' gasped Barnes.

'Whoa! Look at that sucker go!' shouted Hare as the object shot across the clear night sky.

'Tower this is Papa Charlie Alpha One Two One, requesting clearance for… what the hell?'

'Papa Charlie Alpha One Two One. What are you seeing, Casey?' Barnes demanded.

From the cockpit of his DC4 Captain C. S. Pierman reported: 'Tower. They are red turning to white. Tailless. Moving at very high speed. I am seeing about one a minute. That was another. Whatever they are, I am not taking off until the sky is clear.'

'Roger that.'

Harry Truman sat in his robe, in a high-backed armchair, holding a sheaf of briefing papers in one hand, his tin-rimmed glasses in the other. 'Better make it fast or Bess will make your life hell,' he wheezed.

'We have a problem,' said General Twining. 'Visitors. Right over head.'

'How many?'

'Four.'

'Over head? You mean flying around?' Truman cleared his throat. His blue eyes were bloodshot. His shoulders seemed to have narrowed, making him look even smaller than his actual five foot eight.

'No sir. They do not seem to be moving at all.'

'Are they are doing anything that you consider a threat?'

'They have had time to fire if they were hostile. We do not believe they are belligerent at this time.'

'What course of action do you recommend?'

'We should move you, sir.'

'So you think they are a threat?'

'Purely as a precaution.'

'Against what? What's the situation elsewhere? Have they done anything but buzz around?

'Not to our knowledge, sir, but the number of sightings has risen sharply.' Twining opened a manila folder. 'In the past two days we have received reports of 47 sightings in 24 states including D.C. Fourteen were from military observers and six of those were U.S. Air Force bases.'

'You're counting those above us?'

'Those would be in addition.'

'Are all the sightings restricted to the Continental U.S.A?' asked Short.

'No. We have had reports from south of the border, Europe (Germany) and Morocco. A great many sightings are near airports or installations that have some strategic value. They may also be listening to our radio traffic because when we investigate, they disappear only to reappear when we stand down, though not every time.'

The President looked Twining in the eye. 'Has your estimate of the situation changed?'

'No sir. We still believe the visits are extraterrestrial in nature.'

'You don't believe this business of little green men from Mars do you Wallace – General Graham?'

'Like you say, Harry. I've never seen a purple cow and I don't care if I never do,' said Graham. 'Whatever those foo fighters are I would advise against moving you unless you were in clear and present danger.'

Truman turned to Twining. 'General Twining, you have been examining this business for five years. And as far as I'm concerned you still haven't proved your "extraterrestrial hypothesis". But let's just say these phenomena are not natural, how has the situation changed?'

Twining's jaw set. 'In addition to increased activity, we have many recent reports of disks moving at unbelievable speeds. Faster than anything the Reds or we are capable of. Maybe as much as four or even six thousand miles an hour....'

'I have been receiving reports of objects flying at "unbelievable speeds" since the Thunderjet tests at Edwards back in forty-eight or forty-nine; all unproven as far as I can see,' said Truman. 'Look, I don't have a beef against investigating these incidents. It would be negligent not to, even if they all turn out to be sky-hooks or tricks of the light. But critically, not as an act of faith. I have the Lord for that. To be frank, gentlemen, speeds "beyond anything our we or the Reds can come up with" are just that: unbelievable.'

Twining proffered the manila folder.

'You're both airmen,' said Truman, moving his gaze from Twining to Graham and back. 'You know you can't believe your eyes. Even the most experienced pilots make mistakes. So do civilians. Even foot soldiers like yours truly make mistakes.'

'The difference is that we now have many on radar,' Twining announced. 'These sightings and ultra-high speeds are verified and the calculations leave little room for doubt. This is a clear sign of advanced capability.'

Truman took the file and opened it. He scanned the summary and the first two pages, then turned to the final page, skipping about fifteen pages of close-set typing. 'Assuming this is correct, do we have any explanation for this new activity and this flaunting of speed? They are being downright blatant.'

'I believe: communication.'

'They seem to be communicating their presence pretty well.' The President held up a copy of Life. Its cover shot was a picture of Marilyn Monroe, but top right, the cover line read: THERE IS A CASE FOR INTERPLANETARY SAUCERS. 'They're getting more publicity than Ike,' said Truman.

Short winced.

'What do they want to communicate?'

'We have no idea but they may be moving to a new phase. There is a change in pattern. Not only displays of speed but also the static positioning we are seeing overhead. I believe that is a signal.'

'A new phase? And a signal that includes hanging over our heads like that, that Greek myth?' Truman asked wearily.

'The sword of Damocles.' offered Short.

'The sword of Damocles. Yes,' said Truman with rising anger. 'I am staying put, threat or no threat. I have to say, I do not take kindly to any aliens – human, Martian or who knows what – assuming they can freely inhabit U.S. airspace. Particularly the airspace over the Capitol…'

'Sir. If we could make contact…'

'I want you to shoot them down.'

'But we do not know what they are capable of,' said Twining. 'Or what they want.'

'We know what we're capable of,' Truman growled. 'Find out how to do it without putting American lives at jeopardy and shoot them down. Whatever they are. There's an end to it.'

It was still cool but the walk along Pennsylvania Avenue and Fifteenth to the National Press Center had done little to quell the throbbing in Short's temples nor the feeling that his head and shoulders had been welded to form one piece. And he knew that even at this time of the morning the atmosphere in the Tap Room would be thick and laden with smoke, some stale, some still hanging in the air. The sweet smell of pipe smoke hung in the elevator mixed with a musty odor of wood, brass and winter flannel worn in summer. It disgorged Short at the Tap Room's doors. He passed the remnants of an all-night poker game and crossed to a table overlooking F Street. 'Mind if I open this?' he asked the table's sole occupant, a blue-chinned, heavy-set man with a widow's peak of curly hair and dark eyes. Douglas Reeder looked up from an oily cup of Java and a half-full ashtray, folded his copy of the Washington Post. 'Go ahead,' he said. 'Brother, you look beat.'

'Shouldn't you be out talking to some Joe about flying saucers over the Potomac?'

'Sure I should, only I have done eight stories this week on the same subject, and besides even I.N.S. gives us a break to eat some days.'

A white-coated waiter came and stood by the table.

'Two eggs sunny side up. Two for Mister Short, over easy. A fresh coffee and a Bourbon.'

'Thanks.'

'You look like you need it.'

'You don't look so peachy yourself.'

'So what's new?'

'Same old same old.'

'Same old same old don't feed the baby. I heard Harry was sick.'

'You heard wrong.'

'Come on. Give me some credit.'

'That ain't house policy.' Shorty pointed to a sign over the bar.

'Wallace Graham hasn't been seen on the greens at the Burning Tree Club for two weeks. The guy is a golf nut. If the doc ain't around it's because something serious is going on. So what gives?'

'Harry just had the flu but he's as fit as a fiddle.'

'Look me in the eye and say that.'

'As a fiddle.'

'So now he had the flu. How bad?'

'Not bad at all.'

'He's going to have tough time at the convention. You think he's going to run? His popularity is low.'

'You're fishing.'

'So how come he hasn't said a thing about these flying saucers? The whole country's seeing them and they have even been seen over the White House for crying out loud. Not a peep. So we have people wondering if he hasn't made a statement because he is on a trip to Jupiter. Or being held hostage by little green men. '

'Funny. You crack me up. You know all that interplanetary stuff is tripe. The president has not spoken on these fireballs and what-all because there's nothing to say. Some are natural. Some are imaginary. Most are illusions.'

'Says who?'

'We have scientists working on it.' Short could feel his grasp on the exchange slipping. Was he coming down with whatever Harry had?

'Scientists. Atomic scientists?'

'Weather men. Aviation experts. Shrinks.'

'Air Force scientists.'

'No. Well, maybe. Some. A few.'

'The Air Force record sightings, don't they? They keep some kind of book.'

'They investigate incidents, sure, but none of them have panned out. There's nothing that can't be explained. Nothing. In any report.'

'So why do it?'

'They… Why do they do most of the things they do? You were in the service.'

'And no danger or threat from these flying saucers?'

'None whatsoever.'

'Which is why two combat-ready jet fighters were dispatched to National from Newcastle, Delaware at 3 a.m. last night.' He lit a Lucky Strike.

'I can't comment on that.'

'I think you just did. A little bird in the D.C. Air National Guard told me they were F-94s.' He exhaled.

'I am not saying this is the case, in fact anything I say now is off the record, strictly off the record. Number one: was there any action? '

'I heard they skedaddled.'

'There was no action. None,' Short emphasized. 'Whether or not we sent up jets, and whatever their actual mission, if you were to tell the world the U.S. Air Force had just scrambled for a dog fight over the Capitol, you would spark a nationwide panic. Remember Orson Welles? Sure you do. Much beloved of your erstwhile owner William Randolph Hearst. That 'War of the

Worlds' broadcast in thirty-eight created hysteria coast to coast. If you were to put out a story like that, when all this flying saucer baloney died down – and it will because it's horse shit – you would get your statement from the White House. You would get it from Harry S. Truman, personally. He'd say you were the biggest ass in Christendom. He'd say you were un-American. Un-Am-er-i-can. You could not do the enemies of this country a bigger favor at this time than cause panic. Kiss goodbye to your career. Bid sayonara to the International News Service.'

'Say adios, First Amendment.'

'You work – worked – for Hearst, God rot his soul. Don't give me any bull about a free press.'

'Eat your eggs, Shorty.'

'It's been a long night.'

'Sure, Shorty. Eat your eggs.'

Chapter Three
Falling to Earth

Las Vegas, NV. Present.

What could possibly go wrong? Thousands of people have thrown themselves out of a plane from thousands of feet and lived to tell the tale. Mike, Steve, Doug and Gary had undergone almost half a day's solo jump training from guys with wrap-around shades and two-tone hair. They had shout-chanted like mini-Marines – 'One Thousand. Two Thousand. Three Thousand. Four Thousand. Check' – looked up at imaginary failed canopies – scenario: you have a line-over. Nine seconds left. Scenario: the canopy is tangled, you're spinning like a burst tire on the highway, dropping like an anvil. You'll reach a terminal velocity of about one hundred and twenty miles an hour before impact, accelerating at thirty-two feet per second, per second. Scenario: the static line hasn't released correctly and your chute is snagged the tail of the plane: you, the plane, everyone on it will cartwheel into oblivion… The instructor shows you a bowie knife to cut the line. How long to manually deploy the reserve? Six, five. Whoomph. It's up. Round and sound. Check above. Check below. Orientate. The ground rushes into focus. Turn. Knees together. Bend a little. Fists raised to protect the head. Hit the rubber mat. Roll. Stand. Get to the back of the line. Start over.

'You don't count, dude,' said the instructor. Gary,

short, ginger-haired and slightly porky, suspected that had always been the case but was surprised to hear it said quite so directly. His brain and stomach simultaneously flip-flopped, while he rummaged for a reply. He could see two iridescent images of himself floundering in the wrap-arounds. 'You gotta holler, dude.' said the instructor. 'You got to shout it out loud. That way you know you've done your count and so do we. We have to be confident we can take you up because when you're up there's only one way you're coming down, even if we have to kick your ass or shake you off the wing.'

Gary's temporary relief evaporated. He turned to Mike. 'Your idea or mine?'

'Yours buddy. I was all for fishing in Massachusetts Bay. You get to do guy stuff and bring back a shark.'

After the jump and the adrenaline had worn off and they had returned the chutes for packing, Mike was left thinking about the peace he had found briefly between leaving go the wing and the ground coming into sharp focus before he turned and rolled. Even the whooping from above as Gary's canopy had opened could not dispel the wave of calm he felt as he tugged on a line and revolved slowly, quietly above the huge circle of land, the filament of road Duck Taped to it by the little airfield.

As they drove away, Gary rested his elbow on the ledge and steered the black Cadillac with two fingers. 'Pretty cool, huh?' he said looking round to Steve on his right.

'Not as cool as the Fifty-Six model,' said Doug.

'Oh, yeah.' agreed Steve.

'When were you in a Fifty-Six Eldorado?' asked Mike.

'Havana.'

'You were in Havana?' Steve asked. 'Havana, Cuba?'

'Havana, New York. Of course, Havana, Cuba.'

'Beautiful curvy lines. Highly desirable.'

'We're still talking about a car, right?' said Steve.

'And they do a pretty mean cigar,' said Doug producing a ridged leather cigar case from the inside pocket of his jacket. 'Coronas, gentlemen?' he said, offering them around.

'But guys, this is pretty cool,' Gary started again, pressing the lighter on the dash.

'Agreed. The seventy six Caddy Eldorado is, indeed, a classic. Five hundred cubic inch, eight point two liter, vee-eight engine,' said Doug. 'Four hundred B.H.P. Five-fifty foot-pounds of torque.'

'Is that right?' gasped Gary. 'Is he right?'

'Sure he is,' chimed in Steve. 'You mean you didn't know that?'

'Three speed transmission. Disc brakes. One hundred twenty six-inch wheelbase.'

'That is pretty damn impressive. Did your famous granddaddy own one or maybe you just memorized every automobile ever made in the U.S.A?'

'Oh, you know,' said Doug modestly.

Steve grabbed Doug's cell phone and held it in front of Gary so that he could see its screen with the Wikipedia page still open.

'That's research,' said Doug.

'No, that's bullshit!' said Gary, 'But good bullshit. You really had me there for a minute.'

Mike lit Gary's cigar for him, inhaled and coughed. 'Christ on a bicycle. If these are Cuba's finest, bring back the embargo. Here take this.' Cough. 'I don't like to put a damper on this guys but we need to refuel the first chance we get. This is definitely a cool car but it's like a tennis court on wheels and we are, you know, headed out into the desert.'

'What is the limey saying?' demanded Steve.

'I thought I was speaking English. I forgot I still need a translator even after a decade here,' wheezed Mike. 'That has to have been rolled from camel dung. How big's the tank?'

Steve stroked the phone's small screen. 'It's 28 gallons. At, say, 14 miles to the gallon, that's…'

'Three hundred and ninety two miles,' Mike interrupted..

'Way to go, Einstein. We got plenty if we stop at Alamo.'

'We'd better…' said Gary. '…Remember the Alamo!' they all chorused.

'Head for the hills my man,' said Doug imperiously. 'We have an appointment with an alien!'

The long black car breezed along the Great Basin Highway, the land beneath it imperceptibly rising, the patent leather shine of the polished paintwork gradually dulling under a fine film of gray-brown desert dust. The empty landscape became a blur of rocks and sagebrush, punctured by the occasional flash from a discarded can or bottle at the roadside.

'We have officially dropped off the planet,' Doug announced, waving the phone. 'No signal.'

'From now on it's every man for himself. If we run out of food I guess we'll have to eat you Gary,' said Steve.

'Why me?'

'You got the most meat on you, man.'

'I'll remember your kindness and humanity as long as I live.'

'Damn. I meant to phone Jemma,' said Mike.

Gary mimicked the crack of a whip. 'Boy, you've got it bad. You've only been away two days.'

'There'll be a pay phone at Alamo. You can call while we fill up. Let her know you're not being hosed off the runway after your jump,' said Steve.

'If she's like my ex she'll either wonder what you're covering up… or why you're checking up on her,' said Gary.

'You have an ex?' said Doug. 'You old dog.'

'She is seriously paranoid and into all this alien shit. It drove me nuts.'

'If you're not into "all this alien shit", are we heading in the right direction? We're spending the night at Soledad Springs, gateway to the Universe, where U.F.O.s fly through for a Happy Meal before heading off to Uranus.'

'Loony-verse more like.'

'I thought it was your idea.'

'No. It was my idea,' Steve admitted. 'I thought it would be cathartic for Gary – or at least give him some ammunition the next time crazy Becca comes by to liberate some piece of crud they supposedly bought together.'

'Whoa, man! You are bitter. That is definitely transference,' said Mike.

'Men are from Mars, Women are from Venus or some such crap,' Steve replied.

'If they were, it would make Becca easier to explain,' laughed Gary.

At Alamo, they filled up with gas while Mike got change for his call and Steve bought a pair of baseball caps with E.T. printed on them in silver. As Mike relayed news of his continued existence, Steve planted one of the caps on his head. 'Phone home,' he piped. Mike smiled. Steve could hear Jemma talking to Mike, she was not altogether happy if the tone and pitch of her voice were a guide. 'I am getting too old for this kind of weekend and after what happened in Colorado I know it's too tough on you. Maybe it's time I grew up, baby,' said Mike. Jemma replied, then Mike began again. 'I am doing this for me too. I have to go now.'

'There you go. Just what you always wanted,' Steve said, handing Gary the other cap.

'Don't I get one?' asked Doug pulling a face.

'One guy in a hat is wearing a present from the kids. Two look like a couple,' Steve explained. 'If we all had them we'd be a shriners' convention and if it was only me without a hat, I'd look like the loser.'

'Alienated, maybe?' said Doug. 'There's certainly a whole different world inside that head of yours.'

They drove for another 40 miles along the 'Extraterrestrial Highway,' until they reached Soledad Springs and saw the Space Station on the left. The main building was a long, whitewashed, single-story hut with a mural of a waving alien on one side, silver skinned and pop-eyed, and a sign welcoming humans. This was the bar-cum-diner. Behind it were an array of trailers – the motel accommodation – and a few RVs parked up, some more permanently than others. A silver six-wheel trailer sported a tall whip aerial and a Soviet trawler's worth of dishes, air con and solar panels. That was not just the Space Station but also the sum total of Soledad Springs. A dirt road led off from the main highway across the flat brown terrain of the range, towards Bald Mountain. Gary drew into the area indicated by another sign reading 'Park all craft here', and pulled up next to a couple of battered trucks. Doug, Steve and Mike stretched their legs while Gary entered the cabin and was greeted at reception by a woman of anywhere between forty and sixty years. She and Gary had had similar colored hair, except hers was crinkly and a bit grayer, and she weighed about sixty pounds more. Muffin tops breached her bulging blue jeans, topped by a green vest bearing the message 'You can't afford me'. Gary noted that she was also curiously pale for a woman who lived in the desert.

'Why, good afternoon to you,' she said. 'Welcome to the Space Station.'

'Hi. How you doing?' he replied.

'Love your hat,' she said. 'Got plenty more, better if you want them.'

'I'll take a look. Later. Got room for four?'

'Want to double up?'

'Sure.'

She pushed the keys to two trailers across the desk.

'One and seven. They're both pretty much the same. How about a coffee cup?' indicating shelves stacked with posters, T-shirts, masks and green-faced dolls. To the side of the shop Gary could see the bar. It was harshly lit with strip lights that gave the Formica tables and plastic seats an oddly flat appearance. The bar front was airbrushed with clashing planets and exploding stars like the cover of a prog rock album. Above were ranks of dollar bills and notes in exotic currencies that he assumed had been donated by tourists. A line of gambling machines blinked and twinkled along one wall and two men in army surplus combats and plaid shirts played pool.

'If you see lights in the night, stay inside and don't look out the windows,' said the woman.

'You're kidding me,' said Gary.

'Sure I am. Course you can take a peek. You got your cameras with you in case of a sighting? We got video cams. '

'We're good, thanks,' said Gary.

'A lady sold some pictures of a U.F.O. landing to the National Enquirer a year or two back. Bought a fancy car like yours,' she added, looking past them to the Caddy.

'No, really. I'll use the camera on my cell.'

'OK,' she said resignedly. 'You'll need to pay up front. In case of abductions.'

'Sure,' laughed Gary.

'Seriously,' she said.

Later, as the four friends drank beer from the can and waited with mock apprehension for 'alien burgers', the two locals playing pool finally finished their game and came to the bar. The winner, a lanky man with a shaven head and chest-length goatee had triumphed despite sinking an impressive amount of Jack Daniels, pouring and taking swigs between shots. He swayed slightly while the other, squat and dark-eyed, handed over a small sheaf of bills.

‘There goes my profit,’ said the short man darting a glance at his wife, the owner. She replied with a gorgon-like stare.

‘That’s what you’ve got ahead of you,’ Gary whispered to Mike. ‘It’s not too late.’

‘Oh, it is,’ said Doug.

A third man entered: rugged, with a week’s graying stubble and wind-burned cheeks, also in old combats.

‘You fellows ready?’ he said to the two players.

‘Sure. You got a kill?’

‘Four point bull.’

‘I thought you was after big horn,’ chuckled the loser.

‘That’s the official term,’ brayed the lanky player, his laughter cut short as he caught an involuntary glance from Steve.

‘So? You coming, Ray?’ demanded the hunter.

‘Lead the way Jackson,’ said the short man. ‘You know what they say: “Your friends will help you move but your real friends will help you move the body”.’

Steve watched out of the window as the men lifted a tarp from the back of an old, red Sierra four by four flatbed. The vehicle had a line of huge spotlights on the top of the cab and a rusted hood that must have been in a fire sometime. Beside a long coil of half-inch rope and some pulleys lay the remains of a large elk, its blood matt black between the ridges of the worn metal, its head and horns looking startled on its hide, which was wedged between two large lockers.

'I boned the meat where I shot it,' Steve could hear him say. 'It's in the cool boxes. There's about 120 pounds there. I'll take those and you take the legs. I need those boxes empty. '

'You going out again?' said the short man.

'You ain't used all your tags?' asked Lanky.

'I don't need tags for what I'm going after,' said the hunter. 'And I don't mean no ring-tailed cat.'

Steve realized his eavesdropping would be unwelcome. 'You ever filmed in Nevada?' he asked Doug. 'For Nature or P.B.S?'

'No. I guess there would be potential, but there is all over this great land of ours, at least for now. You ever read 'The Last of the Mohicans' – James Fennimore Cooper? He wrote it in about the 1840s and set it in 1757 and he was talking about us destroying the environment even then. '

'Last time I looked we still had an environment,' said Gary, who was beginning to feel the effects of the brew and getting testy.

'If you landed here from outer space you would wonder what the human race was doing letting the planet go hell in a hand basket,' said Doug, 'When we manage to completely destroy the rain forest we'll have lost most of the species on Earth without even knowing what they are; there are plastic garbage patches the size of Texas floating in all our major oceans and we're about to start a war over the oil under the Arctic.'

'You guys are getting way too serious,' said Gary, slurring slightly and passing gas. He turned to see that Ray was behind the bar. Their labors over, the hunter and Lanky were settling on a pair of stools close by, expectantly. Gary signaled to the barkeep: 'Beer me up Scotty,' he grinned.

'You fellas hoping for a sighting?' said Ray, sliding a couple of cans over to his buddies.

'The only way that will happen is if I get another beer or eight,' Gary laughed. He turned to Steve and said in a stage whisper, 'I know they make a living out of tourist crap but even they must know this whole space alien stuff is a crock of shit.'

'There is no need for cussing,' said the red haired woman, bristling.

'What the hell you here for anyway if you don't expect to see nothing?' said Lanky, rearing from his stool.

'Steady, fella,' said Mike. 'He has had a few. He's mostly harmless.'

'No. No, fair play,' said Gary, warming up. 'There is shit all else to do in a shit hole like this than sit around and make up shit and gouge any goddam gullible tourist stupid enough to get off a bus here. Oh look, out there. A space-themed trailer park. It's life Jim, but not as we know it. Thank the Lord.'

'Steady Gary,' said Steve. Lanky took on the demeanor of a crocodile forming the intention to strike but before he could, another man settled on the stool directly between him and Gary.

'Evening, Ray, Marlene,' said the newcomer. 'Beautiful night for it, ain't it?'

Presented with a human barrier, Lanky swayed and looked dumb. Gary looked down at the bar, adrenaline replacing alcohol.

'Get in the truck,' said the hunter to Lanky, 'I'll drop you back.' As he guided Lanky away from the bar he shoulder-barged Gary, shuffling him back a few steps. Doug put his hand on Gary's shoulder to steady him. Mike and Steve stood their ground.

'The better part of valor is discretion,' said Doug, as Gary took an embarrassed pull at his can.

Doug stretched a hand to the new man. 'Doug Reeder.'

Bob Tilson introduced himself. Doug guessed he was about sixty. He had a full head of black hair and a patchy mustache, also still black, and wore gold-rimmed aviator glasses with scuffs on one lens where an arm had rubbed. The glasses gave his head a kind of cubic look. Doug guessed here was some Native American in there.

Mike did the honors for the others. The red-haired woman glared sullenly and the short man went back to the pool table to practice.

'Say, You're the T.V. guy right?' Bob asked, smiling broadly. 'Love your shows, man. I watch all kinds of science. You here to work?'

'No, pleasure. Steve here had some crazy idea we might all see a U.F.O. The original idea was for us to be sipping whiskey and playing Black Jack but my friend the Rain Man, here,' indicating Mike, 'got himself noticed counting cards in two places and we were politely asked to leave.'

'It's not counting, it's working the probability,' said Mike.

'Which we took to mean, leave Las Vegas, although I think we have probably watched too many movies,' said Steve. 'Plan B was a parachute jump and alien-spotting. That was my idea and I apologize to one and all,' said Steve.

'You may think it's all B.S. but people round here do take it seriously and they should,' Bob said to Gary. 'I know these parts and I have seen a lot of things that can't be explained in the normal way of things. You got a lot of government land and genuine military testing sites here which explains some sightings but there's also plenty that can't be written off so easily. I don't just mean lights in the sky, neither.'

Steve looked at him in the non-committal way that a polite arrival reacts to a Krishna panhandling at the airport, hyper-aware of time passing. Gary scowled.

'Suppose there is something out there,' said Doug. 'There's a hundred billion galaxies we know of.

Why, of all the billions of planets in this galaxy, do they visit this one?'

'Last gas for a million light years,' said Mike.

'You got it,' said Bob.

The moon was full and a frigid wind blew. The hunter's flatbed was parked about a hundred yards to his rear against the supplicant branches of a Joshua tree and close to the broken fence that divided civilian from military, forbidden territory. The sky was awash with stars. He moved forward gingerly and knelt. The diffuse, gray-blue moonlight made it hard to tell a razor-sharp rock from a rabbit hole. The hunter had the safety off on his Remington 700 and a .300 round in the chamber. He was about two hundred fifty yards away from what might have been a badger or a fox but he hoped was something much more extraordinary and valuable. Although the hunter's mesopic vision was more acute than most men's after years of twilight forays, his eyesight was no match for that of the creature he was trying to discern. It could see his body heat against the cold stone and dirt as well as if he were standing under a street lamp. Even the residual heat of the truck's engine gave its surroundings a gentle flush. The hunter could hear his prey moving away as he advanced. It was keeping its distance. He carefully reached into his vest pocket for a dog whistle. The prey continued slowly to the ridge but there was no silhouette. The hunter blew the whistle and his quarry stopped in its tracks and stood bolt upright, its torso and head monetarily blocking the subtle star light. He had the spilt second he needed to aim and fire. As the shot rang out he detected a brisk movement through the sage and heard rocks sent tumbling. He edged forward until he reached the spot where he hoped to find his kill. Even in the murk it was plain there was no creature there, neither injured nor dead. He felt around. While there was no blood, the broken twigs and odor of creosote leaves were proof enough that something had fled that spot. And there was a feeling, one he had encountered before: the very real sensation of being watched. But he knew from similar encounters that tonight's hunt was over. He turned in the direction of the fence and back to the Sierra.

Gary needed to sober up some. Doug and Steve were happy to get outside and do some star-gazing. It was a big sky. Bob pointed them in the right direction and wished them luck. Mike led the way with a flashlight in one hand and a flat of beers under one arm. They had come out of the Space Station's ice box with little likelihood of their getting warm out there. Any heat in the ground had gone straight up into the night. Mike and Doug talked about orbital resonance and why using it was the best hope of identifying another planet that could support life. Steve and Gary left them to the discussion. When they had gotten far enough from the Space Station to ignore its glow they parked themselves on a hummock and began to scan the sky and the hills.

Steve said to Mike, 'I know I'm going to regret this but what the hell were you and Doug talking about?'

Just as Mike geared up to explain how cosmologists might use math to identify a stable planetary system, Gary gasped. 'There's a light over where Bob said,' he whispered. And sure enough, there was a small stationary blob of white light a mile or so distant above the side of the mountain like a low, bright star.

'Well, I guess I was wrong,' said Gary. 'My apologies to Becca.'

Steve snorted.

'I do kind of miss her,' said Gary.

'You poor sap,' said Steve, and patted him on his shoulder.

On the mountainside, the hunter was overcome with fear. He found himself running, involuntarily clattering through the brush and scrambling headlong over the rocks, driven by a thunderous noise and a blinding light from above. He slipped in a rabbit run and barreled forward, crashing headlong into a wall of rock. His breath burnt in his chest. He clawed at the brittle surface, scrambled upright. The light encircled him again. He felt nausea, then searing pain. He convulsed: a fish in the air. Blood spurted from his nostrils and mouth. His bowels and bladder burst, soaking his pants in mucus and feces. His skin swelled and rippled. Then he slumped like a circus tent. Dead.

The helicopter remained overhead with its spotlight trained on the corpse, as it hoisted up an object the size of a trash can. The narrowband sonic device it hauled had tuned into the natural frequency of the hunter's skeleton, pulsing rhythmically but inaudibly so the whole framework became elastic, flexing and contorting as if a Mexican wave were running through it in all directions; it sheared soft tissue and organs, until the oscillating halted and the buckled bones shattered.

A small group of soldiers was already making its way towards the dead man. When they reached the foot of the wall they took the slack sack of molten human and slipped it into a body bag, then carried it to where the bag could be lifted into the helicopter. As it clattered away, they looked for the rifle and the spent cartridge. Two of them forced back the fencing and then returned to the Sierra. One got in and popped the hood, the other reached in and started the motor. As they drove it away its taillights glowed palely in the light of a false dawn, and the hunter's prey fled the mountain.

The four friends fell into silence and the kind of calm that is only possible in nature. It could have been 20 minutes or a whole hour later when Gary was the first to stir. He lit a cigarette, inhaled and then let it burn between his fingers, his hands crossed over his knees. It signaled a general stirring, like a herd becoming unsettled. Doug stood and stamped his feet. 'Must be the cigarette smoke,' said Mike. Then, in a pukka

English accent: 'Light the blue touch paper and retire. I am off to ablute, gentlemen. I may be some time.'

Steve gave him the tissue he had folded up and stuffed into his back pocket and Gary handed him his lighter adding: 'Don't set fire to the place,' said Steve. 'And go down wind.'

The search for privacy took Mike a good distance from the others. He found an arroyo and followed it. Its dry bed, free from vegetation was ideal for the purpose and whatever was left behind could be covered by a rock. But when he stopped, he heard a noise. Like a kitten. Somewhere close but muffled like it was trapped behind a wall. He followed the sound, until he came across a bank with a dry gully defined by shadow. Against the black there was what looked curiously like water. Not ice but not static. As he got closer he saw a bundle of reflective fabric, like a space blanket. The sound came from within. He reached down gingerly to pull the fabric away and it moved.

Mike's instincts made him leap back. Then he began to understand what he was actually seeing. It was a child. A ghostly white face the size of the palm of his hand looked up at him. In the half-light, its eyes looked huge. They were like wrap-around sunglasses, but real eyes. He see them staring at him. The mewing stopped. The child struggled but could not free itself from where it was wedged.

'Steady,' said Mike, 'Steady.' And he knelt down putting hand beneath the child's head and down below it shoulders, He used the other hand to push between its shoulder and the side of the crack and, with a tug, freed it. In that light, the child looked odd indeed. Almost as if it were starving, a big stary-eyed head on a fragile body wrapped in foil. It remained there, quite clearly petrified. Mike went to check that nothing was broken but it shrank away.

'O.K. O.K. You're fine now. We'll find someone and take you home,' Mike said, gently.

But something in the child's strange eyes made him turn. He looked up to see someone very tall and thin looming over him. He wore white. Almost anyone but Mike would have thought it was an angel. An angel of death. Mike felt a terrible, scalding pain across his chest and face. He staggered and collapsed, landing hard on his side next to the child. The angel shimmered above him. He was going to strike again and Mike could do nothing to avoid it.

He was paralyzed. Immobile and helpless, he could only wait for the next strike.

A toxic mix of fear and anger, red fury at facing death with so much more to do, flooded his brain. He struggled within as if he was wrenching himself awake but the nightmare was real. He strained. He tried to cry out. Nothing. His senses began to fill. He heard a loud rushing, and saw a blinding light.

Then, a second figure appeared between Mike and the assailant who had so effectively incapacitated him. He saw it bow over the child and lift it up. The two figures turned without a sound and carried the child away.

Mike lay there locked-in, voiceless, barely able to breathe. He fainted away.

When Mike woke, the sun was up and he was looking at… Steve.

Steve told him that he and Doug and Gary had got worried. Doug had organized them to search for Mike using what they had all learned in Scuba. Assuming Mike had not doubled back they could fan out at roughly sixty degree angles and then search in a growing spiral, counting their paces and adding another five before each turn. It would soon be dawn, which would help. Steve had just paced out a hundred and was about to turn to his right again when he saw a movement. It looked for all the world like the horses he had once seen galloping through the marshes in the Carmargue, pale and fast, far faster than a running man. Then, without knowing why, he retraced his steps and jumped down into the arroyo. What he had mistaken for a boulder was Mike.

With effort, they got Mike to his feet and began to stumble together in the direction of the Space Station, whose low buildings and vehicles were still black against the warming sky.

'I thought we'd never find you. You can't make a habit of this Mike,' puffed Steve.' The guys have been looking for you for half the night. 'It's like the goddam avalanche all over again. Man, it's good to see you, though. I don't know how you did it at night, buddy, but you have all the symptoms of heat stroke. When we get you back to the Space Station we'll get some ice.'

At first Mike was dead weight but very soon the headache and nausea subsided and the trembling stopped. His walking became surer and all the while Mike could smell the early morning desert and it made him thankful to be alive. By the time they reached the Space Station, Mike had not only almost completely recovered but, if anything, was beginning to experience something approaching ecstasy – a weird, inexplicable feeling of beneficence and well-being.

Steve eyed him with concern. He had seen Mike like this once before and he had gone missing then too. It wasn't a form of attention seeking behavior. Not with Mike. The guy had been in real bad shape less than half an hour ago. Yet here he was, practically radiating – like before, like when they pulled him from the snow. If it was psychosomatic, Steve had never come across anything like it in the text books. When they got back to Boston. Mike, not entirely metaphorically, was going under the microscope.

'What happened out there buddy?' Steve asked as they entered the Space Station.

'I don't know,' Mike replied. 'Something.'

'Oh looky here,' said the red-haired woman. 'You couldn't have had a close encounter by any chance?'

The next day, Mike was fine. Better than fine. The others, less so. So he took the wheel and drove them back to Vegas. At McCarran, they found a place for steak and coffee. Steve and Doug's flight was scheduled an hour before the other pair's, which is why it was not until after they landed in Boston that they learned that Mike and Gary's plane had crashed.

Colonel Zephram Baxter preferred to drive his own vehicle, a British Jaguar X-Type, so he was easy for the dogged clutch of perennial anti-drone protesters at the side of Highway 95 to spot. He recognized them, too: the old hippy with the prophet beard; the bony woman, the fat daughter – and the banner. 'U.S. drone wars terrorism'. They had held it up every day for four years, undisturbed and ignored except when a T.V. station needed footage of kooks or pinkos. As he passed the sign to the now demolished Indian Springs Casino and gas station and he turned into the main gate to Creech Air Force Base, the familiar thought crossed his mind that if they only knew what he really did to protect their liberal asses they would be too busy pissing in their pants to protest. The trio had become such a feature he had forgotten they worked for Uncle Sam: a lure for itinerant troublemakers and visible proof to the half-hearted that someone more committed was on the case.

There was the thump of ordnance on the test ranges as Baxter parked the Jag and walked over to the nondescript building that was home to the 'chair force'. It housed the ground control stations where Predator and MQ-9 Reaper drones were guided to killing fields thousands of miles distant. On each side of the unmarked corridor there were small rooms closely packed with screens, consoles and servers, where shift-working drone pilots and sensor operators watched and, when ordered, struck. Baxter knew there was a morale problem caused by boredom and burnout. The rooms crammed with kit might look like simulators but the combat was real. And killing, even at a distance, combined with the banalities of suburban family life off-base – weekend tailgate parties and barbecues, TV, chores and all – and the need for secrecy, even with partners, created a special sort of stress. Baxter could almost taste it in the air as he reached the classified section and entered the G.C.S. where Major Kirby waited. He only wanted good news.

Kirby saluted. 'Take a look at this, general,' she said. 'The thermal images from the breach incident show how effective the Coyame device is at segregating targets.' She ran a video of two shimmering black and white figures moving against a gray background: the hunter and his prey. 'You'll see they have different thermal profiles. Our man is a darker and cooler, at least until he starts running. Structurally they are very similar apart from the skull and the maxillary orbits, the eye sockets, but not so close that the device affects them both. We have seen this with cattle, pigs and we tried it on other mammals we acquired when the zoo closed – all using corpses – but this is the first trial with a live subject and the first time we have used it with a visitor present as a control.'

‘Did we put the visitor there?’

‘No.’

‘Thank the Lord.’

‘The young ones like to roam beyond the inner perimeter. I’m guessing this is a favorite route. That would explain why the intruder has returned to the same area regularly, on or close to the full moon.’

‘Was the visitor hurt?’

‘There’s no evidence either on the ground or from the video and we have not received any advice to that effect. We were primarily concerned with bringing the intruder in for autopsy.’

‘That’s good. Deal with it through liaison and let me know if there is any blowback. What about the autopsy?’

‘As predicted, so far. Compound and hair fractures of all the major bone mass; cranial plates separated and misaligned; internal organs shredded,’ said Kirby. ‘After ninety seconds exposure, the guy was chowder.’

‘We need to test this with armor, in vehicles, through walls. This has more practical potential than the neutron bomb: zero radiation and everything other than the target left intact and undamaged. If we can develop a reliable means of delivery… ‘

‘We have a small multi-rotor U.A.V. on order that will take a payload of sixteen pounds. That’s more than we need to take a device into the mountains and lower it into a cave or a gully, kill the bad guys and then recover any Intel material at our leisure. Now we have the detection and analysis algorithms, body mass and so on, we can step up the testing.'

'If we get the analysis right it could help us solve our other problem,' Baxter mused. As senior staff officer Kirby was itching to exchange her gold oak leaf for a silver lieutenant colonel's. When she had called Baxter he had made it clear that the way the morning's' events turned out would determine whether she would achieve her aim of joining the general staff. Things were looking pretty damn chipper. Until the klaxon rasped into life.

The siren was steady. So not an attack. The Big Voice barked: 'Strike on installation. This is not a drill. First responders to stations. This is not a drill.'

Before she had even heard it ring, Kirby lifted the receiver. 'Type two emergency. Civilian strike. Smoking hole. On installation. Northeast quadrant,' she relayed.

Kirby slammed down the receiver and sped to the pre-designated incident control center. Baxter followed on at a brisk, controlled pace. Men and women ran to their positions. Four massive P-22 pumpers and a pair of P30 rescue trucks emerged from the firehouse and headed towards the black tower of smoke to the north, tailed by an assortment of Hummers, trucks and ambulances. The base siren died down while the vehicles' wailed in a fading cacophony.

'Get me eyes,' Kirby snapped to the team already assembled in the emergency operations center. 'I want a full assessment. And set up a cordon, immediately. Get everybody on base. Prioritize the D.R.F. You have their names.'

'We have Lincoln County on the line. Do we require assistance?' shouted Staff Sergeant Lemual 'Lemmy' Medlar.

'Have them on stand-by,' barked Kirby. 'But notify all the local civil authorities that the incident is on installation and we believe there in no hazard, repeat no hazard, to the civilian community. We are assessing. If we need assistance, we will inform them.'

Colonel Baxter entered with General Snow. 'You the I.C?' Snow demanded.

'Yes sir.'

'Give me a sit rep.'

Kirby turned to Lemmy. 'Staff Sergeant.'

'Civilian Boeing seven three seven out of L.A.S. to Boston. A hundred and thirty, one three zero passengers and eight crew. According to the tower there was an I.R.S. malfunction shortly after takeoff.'

'Who do you have as S.M.R?' asked Baxter.

'Briggs can handle the media,' she replied. 'Medlar. Have the perimeter along that quadrant checked. Call the sheriff and get him to put men on his side of the gates in case we have to chase anyone off, and organize a C2 close to the strike location, with full communications. Determine a hot zone and set up a field hospital outside it for any survivors who can't be moved immediately.'

'You're not keeping C2 here?' asked Snow.

'When they have comms and we have more detailed assessment we'll move command and control in as close as we can,' she replied. 'The strike is midway between here and Area S-4.'

'I don't need to emphasize how important awareness of the situation is with regards to the Visitors.'

'Yes, General. As soon as we have established hot and warm zones our people will cordon off the approach to Area S-4. The perimeter is sealed. We may need civilian responders on the main strike site and for immediate retrieval.'

'Keep me informed at all times,' said Snow.

As the general left, an airman first class saluted Kirby and handed her a note. 'Oh Christ,' she said and passed it to Baxter. It read: 'Strike due near-collision A.S.C.'

'Mother of God,' said Baxter. 'What in Sam Hill was an alien scout craft doing over Las Vegas? Contact the D.C.I. immediately. We need N.S.A. to monitor the social media. Get Briggs in here. The navigation error cover won't hold for long. We need a plausible alternative: a rogue test drone.'

'Blame it on a rogue drone, a month before a Federal budget review?' said Kirby incredulously.

'We're flying fifty missions a day from here. We are not going to lose our funding. But, you're right, we had better make it a light aircraft. Civilian. Buy one if you have to. Meanwhile we need the voice and data boxes A.S.A.P. Military investigators only. Do we have someone inside the F.A.A. we can rely on when it comes to the report?'

'Affirmative,' answered Kirby. Baxter shredded the note. 'Contain the source of that report,' he ordered.

'Total secrecy. Nothing electronic.'

The red line rang. 'Sir,' said Kirby, holding out the phone's mouthpiece. 'It's the President.'

'Put him on hold.' Baxter snapped. He was already on another scrambled line. 'This is Colonel Zephram Baxter. Mike. Juliet. Seven. Seven. One. Seven. We have a Code Majestic.'

Chapter Four
Contact

Washington D.C. 1953

Eisenhower stood on the veranda of the Oval office. The damp February air and the deep chill reflected his mood. At two minutes before ten the alarm on his Vulcain Cricket sounded. Without glancing at the wristwatch he turned and pulled the glass-paned door behind him. As he positioned himself behind the broad desk, an inner door opened.

'The Director of Central Intelligence,' said an aide.

'Send him in,' Eisenhower said, barely raising his gaze from the file he was now reading.

'Mister President,' said General Walter 'Beetle' Bedell Smith, extending a hand across the desk he thought of as Harry S. Truman's. Eisenhower remained seated. After so many Friday intelligence meetings with Truman, and even after the briefings Harry had insisted be given to candidates, it still seemed odd to Smith to see The Old Man at the helm.

Neither had aged much in the eight years since Smith had been his hatchet man at Supreme Headquarters Allied Expeditionary Force and had signed the German Instrument of Surrender on Ike's behalf. Ike still had the deceptive appearance of a bemused hare. Smith's slicked back hair and high forehead, combined with deep ridges in his cheeks and a cleft chin gave him an altogether harsher look that belied his ability to deploy charm, when necessary. Despite their civilian garb both men still had the carriage of high-ranking officers.

'You may sit,' said Ike. 'I have been catching up. Harry Truman gave you a poisoned chalice. I know you were not any happier to take on the post of D.C.I. than either of your predecessors. '

Ike was right. Smith had not wanted the job and between his accepting it in May and talking up the role in October, there had been an all mighty intelligence failure that was still reverberating around the world: the communist invasion of South Korea. For all anyone knew, it signaled the start of the Third World War. The fact that the C.I.A. was taken by surprise confirmed everything that the Intelligence Survey Group's report had said about its lack of coordination, poor intelligence-gathering and internal feuds.

'Typical of the man to create such as mess,' Eisenhower continued. 'You know I wanted you as my chief of staff when Truman made me Supreme Allied Commander Europe? He said you were too important as D.C.I.'

Smith knew this and that President Truman and General Eisenhower had once been close enough for Truman to offer to run with The Old Man on the same ticket – as Ike's deputy president. Truman was a Democrat through and through, a party stalwart and a loyalist. He knew Ike was, effectively, non-partisan and that Ike had based his decision to accept the Republican nomination on an assessment of Harry's declining appeal to voters. That had not hurt Harry as much as Ike's characterizing him as inept at home and useless abroad, particularly since they had seemed to agree completely on foreign policy up to that point. Truman was disgusted that Ike had caved in to pressure from Joe McCarthy and denounced George Marshall as a communist. Marshall was the man Ike had narrowly beaten to the role of Supreme Allied Commander and whose plan for reconstruction had been, in Truman's mind, the only and most effective bulwark against the Soviets in Europe, other than the A-bomb.

The ice had entombed their relationship by the time they had ridden together as president and president-elect to Eisenhower's inauguration ceremonies, late last month. Smith also suspected that as the frost had been forming, he himself had been the focus of a piece of petty wrangling in which Ike had blocked Smith's military promotion until Harry had ordered it forced it through. The thankless task of pulling the intelligence agencies together so that they at least had some coherent ways of working – even just shared the same pay grades – had taken two years of hard slog. And this for the man who had convinced the Nazis to let him through their lines to feed the starving Dutch. Now, he was in the curious position of remaining as D.C.I. but also waiting for the Senate to confirm him as an Under-Secretary of State. A different chalice.

'It's the job I have been given,' said Smith. He noticed Harry had taken the sign with him that said 'The buck stops here.'

'As D.C.I. what is your assessment of the flying disks?' said Ike. For a second, Smith wondered if he had heard right. 'I want to know what is going on.'

'The agency has been monitoring the U.F.O. situation for more than three years now through the Office of Scientific Intelligence and the Office of Current Intelligence,' said Smith, swiftly gathering his thoughts. 'We monitor them through the Air Technical Intelligence Center. Bob Amor, the D.D.I., has been looking at the defense and national security implications. The agency believes that although the vast majority can be explained as natural phenomena – there is only a one in one hundred thousand likelihood that they pose a threat – we need more resources and manpower to be sure though and explain them all. To that end, on Four December, the Intelligence Advisory Committee agreed that we should elicit the services of the best qualified scientists to review and appraise the evidence.'

'When are they doing this?'

'The Scientific Advisory Panel on U.F.O.s sat last week. '

'What did they conclude?'

'That there is no threat to the National Security of the United States,' said Smith. 'But there is the danger that a flap over flying disks could throw us off our guard and blind us to any genuine hostile attack by the Soviets.' He paused. 'It is also curious that no sightings have been reported in eastern Europe, which raises the possibility that they are being used for psychological warfare. Marshall Chadwell, our A.D. for Scientific Intelligence believes that a significant number of the population is now so mentally conditioned to accept the incredible that if the Soviets were to mount a surprise attack they would not understand its true nature – and that includes service personnel.'

Smith could see Eisenhower's eyes going black.

Neither man spoke of it but in the fall, Ike had taken part in Exercise Mainbrace. The N.A.T.O. sea maneuvers were a massive operation: N.A.T.O's biggest to date and the largest since World War Two, involving 80,000 men, 200 ships, and 1,000 planes. Ike had flown by chopper to see the exercise taking place under the aegis of the new Allied Command Atlantic at first hand, landing on the U.S.S. Franklin D. Roosevelt at a point midway between the British Isles and Norway. The F.D.R. was the flagship of the U.S. Sixth Fleet and one of 10 aircraft carriers taking part. It had nuclear weapons aboard, as did some of the aircraft on constant maneuvers. This was designed to make it harder for the Reds to keep track of their location and to allow forward basing in the event the Soviets made a move on Western Europe. In retrospect, Ike realized that the scale of the operation and the fact that both the F.D.R. and a number of aircraft taking part were carrying nuclear weapons might be linked to what happened next.

It was stormy. At about 1.30 a.m., Ike rose from his cot and made his way to the Rosie's signal bridge clad in his robe and looking for coffee. A blue light hovered about a hundred feet above the water to starboard. As Ike strained to make out its source, there was a flash of lightening and he could clearly see that it was coming from a metallic disk-shaped object that remained in mid-air as the carrier plowed past.

Smith was aware that Ike was not the only one to have had an encounter at sea but nothing inexplicable had registered on the ship's height-finding or air search radar. Why reach for the most outlandish explanation when what they saw was likely a weather effect or all in the mind? 'There seems little doubt that many sightings result from mass hysteria,' Smith said.

Eisenhower was caught between what he believed and what he prayed was right, but would rather be a fool than look like one. 'What do they recommend?' he asked.

Smith put on a pair of wire-framed glasses and read. 'I quote: "the continued emphasis of the reporting of these phenomena does, in these parlous times, result in a threat to the orderly functioning of the protective organs of the body politic." The panel recommended we "reassure the public of the total lack of evidence of inimical forces behind the phenomena, train personnel to recognize and reject false indications quickly and effectively, and to strengthen regular channels for the evaluation of and prompt rejection to true indications of hostile measures."'

'And you?'

'We need to maintain vigilance but at the same time stop our boys at the Air Bases reporting anything like this to the press, under severe penalty, and that we should undertake, through the press and so on, to neutralize the propaganda effect of civilian sightings. Discredit, ridicule the sources; down play the reports. President Truman brought in Executive Order 9835, which allows us to fire federal employees disloyal to U.S.A. You could extend the loyalty program. And there are always the psych wards.'

'Who are they, this advisory panel?'

'The chairman is a cosmologist from Caltech, H.P. Robertson. He put together a team with Luis Alvarez and Samuel Goudsmit, both geniuses in atomic physics; two astronomers, Hynek and Page; Lloyd Berkner, the engineer, and Frederick C. Durant. Durant was the director of engineering for the Naval Air Rocket Test Station but he is currently a test pilot. All good men. '

'And how long did they take to reach this conclusion?'

'Four days.'

'Four days? I see,' said Eisenhower. 'And who or what is Majestic?'

Shangri-La was only sixty or so miles from Washington but a world away from D.C. Had Smith chosen the location to rile him? Ike has specifically said the Catoctin Mountain compound was a needless luxury, one that was too readily associated with Roosevelt. From the window of the unmarked Lincoln Cosmopolitan that carried him through the bare Maryland woods and the melting snows, Ike had his first view of the main lodge with its shingle roof and smoke rising from the short stone stack. This was fried chicken and mashed potatoes to the fancy French cuisine of the White House, and sure as heck closer to the army man's heart than the politician's. He would give it a stay of execution; change its name. Camp David would do well enough. As the car drew up, a U.S. Marine saluted and stepped forward to open his door.

A dozen men stood or sat around the long broad table in the Laurel Lodge waiting for the President's entrance. General Twining leaned on the mantle of the stone chimney and cast his gaze up to the brass clock at the hub of the capstan wheel mounted above it. The meeting had been set for 13.00 hours and there were two minutes to go. The table was bare. No pads, pencils or name cards. There was silence.

As the President entered with his senior staff assistant, Gordon Cray, and Beetle Smith, the sitting men stood and the others arranged themselves respectfully. 'Mister President' said Smith. 'I will introduce you to the committee and explain its work. You already know General Hoytenburg from his role as Chief of Military Intelligence and as my predecessor as D.C.I. , and Rear Admiral Souers, the first D.C.I., of course. Rear

Admiral Hillenkoetter, former Director of the C.I.A. from 1947 to 1950. Doctor Vannevar Bush is familiar to us all for his outstanding work on the atomic bomb. Doctor Bush is the committee's chairman. General Twining, you know. Doctor Detlev Bronk is president of the National Academy of Sciences; Doctor Jerome Hunsaker, head of the National Advisory Committee on Aeronautics; Doctor Lloyd Birkner…'

Eisenhower broke in. 'Birkner? You are on the U.F.O. panel. Is that right?'

'Yes, sir.'

'And you think they're all bunk?'

'For the most part, yes, but there is a little more to it than that, Mister President.'

'…Major General Montague is the C.O. at White Sands Proving Ground,' continued Smith. 'And, finally, Doctor Donald Menzel is professor of astrophysics and associate director of solar research at Harvard University.'

'Another U.F.O. debunker?' Ike asked.

'I am a scientist,' Bush said in a voice that was clear and warm. 'I am not being facetious when I say I believe unidentified flying objects are simply flying objects whose nature we has not so far been identified. That is all.'

'Mister President, if you would care to sit?' say Cray proffering the armchair at the head of the table. 'Gentlemen.'

'Mister President,' said Bush. 'We are honored that you are here. The timing could not be more appropriate. As you will see, we are on the verge of an event that will change world history and reshape the future of humanity, an era of discovery that will make the scientific and engineering breakthroughs of the last century – aviation, radio, the atom bomb – seem like the first uncertain steps of a toddling child.'

As he spoke, Bush's kindly face lost none of its immediate charm but his soft blue eyes never moved for an instant from the President's. 'I must warn you sir, that as broad and profound as your experience has been in the military field and now as the leader of our great country, dare I say, the Free World, nothing you will have encountered before will prepare you for the revelation – yes, revelation – you are about to receive. May I add that when we embarked on this journey ourselves none of us had even the remotest idea of where it would lead or the extraordinary, unprecedented possibilities it would provide not only for America but the whole of mankind. Perhaps it was fortunate that we had no foreknowledge of the present situation, for if we had, our efforts would surely have been paralyzed by trepidation.'

'We should start at the beginning,' said Smith.

'Indeed,' said Bush, pausing to clean his glasses with a crisp, white kerchief. 'You will be aware, sir, that in 1947 there were reports that a U.F.O. had crashed in New Mexico. I was there. My solar studies frequently take me to Colorado and New Mexico and I was at the Holloman Air Base, near Alamogordo, at the height of the flying-saucer scare. I witnessed what we would call a U.F.O. from the back seat of an automobile. I was admiring the full moon when I noticed a pair of stars. For a moment I thought they might be Castor and Pollox before realizing that it was the wrong time of year. I could not get a clear focus on the two hazy disks of blue light hovering there so we pulled over to get a better look and they flew off as fast and just as mysteriously as they appeared.'

'I had a similar experience at sea,' nodded Ike.

'Yes, sir, I believe you did,' said Bush. 'And you would not have been alone in doing so. But if you are hoping for an explanation I cannot give you one. I can only tell you what I saw. However, a brief while after this sighting I received a long distance call with a request to come to Washington to meet Secretary of Defense James Forrestal. He swore me to secrecy before he revealed why I had been summoned. You, sir, are the first person other than the men around this table, to whom I have revealed any of this. In brief, he asked me to form a special investigative group codenamed Majestic to be established by special classified executive order of President Truman. He charged me with recruiting the other members, all of whom you see before you, plus General Smith who joined after Secretary Forrestal's unfortunate death. All these gentlemen agreed to come on board and maintain strict secrecy, which in the light of immediate events was essential.'

'I respected Forrestal. He was an excellent Secretary for Defense. I do not understand why a man of his capability and presence of mind would kill himself,' said Ike. 'It was a tragedy for the country.'

'President Truman wanted to get to the bottom of a report that a U.F.O. had crashed at Corona, New Mexico, close to Roswell Army Air Force Base. Shortly after my meeting with Secretary Forrestal, we received a further report that the remains of the pilot or crew of the disk had been recovered near the crash site. As unlikely as this eventuality seemed, it could not go un-investigated. General Twining and I reached an initial conclusion confirming that a disk-like aircraft of some kind had crashed and we surmised that it was a short-range reconnaissance vehicle of a type that we were unfamiliar with.'

'You are an Air Force general, Twining. And you did not recognize an aircraft?' Ike demanded testily.

'With respect, sir: I could not identify the wreckage.'

Bush resumed. 'We were provided with a team from an operational detachment of the New Mexico Army National Guard. They were not told what they were doing or why but they were directed to search for remains while the wreckage was taken to a number of locations for analysis.'

'We2 debriefed the rancher and other civilians who had witnessed the craft and the crash,' said Souers. 'The press was told that it was a weather balloon.'

Detlev Bronk leaned forward and ran his fingers along the central parting atop his unusually ovoid head. Ike knew the name but could not place it. He realized with unease that Joseph McCarthy had him figured as a crypto-commie. As little time as Ike had for McCarthy's methods he might be right that communists had permeated the whole of government, academia and Hollywood. Was this some kind of Red cell? Ike began to wonder.

'As a biologist, Mister President, I am aware that Mother Nature has many, many surprises for us, and we have a great deal yet to discover, but I was flummoxed by what I saw on the operating table and under the microscope,' said Bronk, looking up. 'The remains were in a terrible condition. They had been disturbed by desert animals and had obviously also suffered impact. The cellular structure could have come from a number of species but when we tried to piece together the remains we had reluctantly to conclude that these creatures had evolved along a different path to our own. Field studies are notoriously unreliable but these results were so unusual that we felt obliged to categorize them, in other words, as extraterrestrial biological entities.'

'Little green men?'

'Gray, as a matter of fact. Little gray men with very large eyes, as far as we could tell,' said the scientist. 'I cannot tell you the frustration that I have suffered in not being able to share or reveal the discovery of a whole new form of life, beyond this group.'

'Sir, as you may know, I have a great deal of experience of aircraft design,' said Jerome Hunsaker, 'including aerodynamics. At M.I.T. we built a wind tunnel to test wings and other surfaces and we have been trying to develop saucer-like craft with as little wind resistance as possible. If we can reduce the friction, the air we could magnify the velocity of aircraft massively…'

'What Jerome is saying,' General Montague cut in, 'is that we have tried to create something like this flying saucer and failed. We have no idea what propelled it, what the power source was, how it was guided – there are no wires or vacuum tubes – how it flies without any kind of wing. It is – it has to be – extraterrestrial technology. If the Reds had this they would be marching up Pennsylvania Avenue right now.'

Ike looked round the room, from face to face. 'Are you saying President Truman knew that there were real men from Mars here in the U.S.A and did nothing about it?' he asked in disbelief?

'No, sir,' said Admiral Hillenkoetter. 'He made it clear to Forrestal that until and unless it was proven beyond all doubt that flying disks were extraterrestrial, and that they represented a threat, that we should simply carry on investigating and only report a change in status.'

'That Alice in Wonderland logic is probably what drove Forrestal mad,' said Menzel. 'I wonder for my own sanity at times, when I have to deny in public what I fear is true in private.'

Two men in the room knew Forrestal had been administered a hallucinogen before he threw himself out a sixteenth floor window. He had threatened to go public on Majestic.

'Since President Truman received our estimation of the situation in 1947 we have been monitoring and analyzing all U.F.O. incidents in an operation that provides us with more certainty, while preventing a public panic,' said Smith. 'Meanwhile, we have observed the need for secrecy at a level higher even than Top Secret.'

Ike reached back into his memory. Brigadier General Ramey, the head of Eighth Air Force had reported something to him about a B29 taking wreckage from New Mexico to Wright Field in Ohio. The report had been so oblique and so hedged around with talk of balloons for nuclear test monitoring that unless Ike had had today's meeting he might never have understood its significance. Ramey had discharged his duty in informing Ike as Army Chief of Staff but in such as way to obfuscate it completely. Twining,. sitting right there, in front of Ike, had been head of Air Material Command's intelligence and engineering divisions at Wright. Ike had been played in forty-seven and was being treated like a mutt now.

'So secret you kept the President of the United States, your Commander-in-Chief, in the dark?' Ike spat. 'That is damn close to treason. By God, I may put you all before a firing squad. What else are you hiding?'

Bush broke the silence. 'There has been a change is status, Mister President. A momentous one. We have made contact.'

Chapter Five

Missing, presumed alive

Over Illinois. Present

'If I think about what is happening I will go crazy,' said the woman. 'I am not sitting with my husband because he has to go through this every time we fly. I am rattling with tranks but I still feel real bad. I'm sorry to burden you.'

'Fear of flying is rational,' said Steve. 'Flying isn't natural, we have to have machines to do it, like breathing under water, but it is safe.' He looked from her to Jemma, wondering how she held herself together. Mike had just died in a plane. A crash. In a plane. Like this one heading for the same place where his crashed and he died. Christ.

Despite her own outward composure, Jemma could hardly have failed to see the other woman's distress. She, Doug and Steve had grabbed the last seats on the flight and she and Steve had found themselves either side of her, with Jemma in the window seat, Steve on the aisle. Doug was somewhere in back. Inside, Jemma's survival mechanism was to shut down and focus on the hope, the conviction, that somehow Mike had survived. Besides, if she engaged with the woman they would probably spark one another off.

Oddly, they had all discussed the chances of living through a plane crash only weeks before, over linguine and clams at a place in Boston's North End. Doug has been researching the subject for P.B.S. for a program that never got made. The conversation had started with the number of rock stars who had perished in light aircraft, moved on to 'Airport' and 'Snakes on a Plane' via the Bermuda Triangle and then, inevitably, with Mike there, to the odds of surviving various types of aviation disaster. Steve and Gary had joked darkly about the brace position being there so you could kiss your ass goodbye. Mike cited cases where passenger jets had crashed but there had been survivors, usually when a plane had missed the end of the runway and come skidding to halt in jungle, or similar. Ironically, in one case, a man, a soldier, had survived almost unscathed when he was been thrown free on impact, because he was the only one on board not to have fastened his seat belt. In another, a six-year-old girl simply got up from the wreckage of a light aircraft and walked to a nearby farm to ask for help. Now Steve was trawling his memory for Mike's statistics on aircraft safety compared to an assortment of mishaps from shark attacks to lighting strikes and choking on a nut. The woman responded by citing a list of phobias and fears, some her own, others belonging to friends or that she had heard about on T.V. Steve ran his hand over the stubble he had been developing since he had first set off to Vegas with Mike, Gary and Doug, and thanked his lucky stars that pogonophobia wasn't another of her fears.

Shamefully, Steve caught himself thinking that Gary

had very probably perished too, poor guy, but at least no-one had heard from Crazy Becca so she wasn't the one he was talking down. Oddly, the morbid conversation calmed the woman, while Jemma seemed to pick up only bits of it like a shortwave signal wallowing in and out of hearing. And so Steve kept the woman talking right through the landing at McCarran and when she had been reunited with her husband he waited with Jemma at the bridge, until Doug joined them.

'Hertz rental. Corporate account,' said Doug briskly. He signed for a Kia Rio and took the Las Vegas freeway, passing the back of the despised Bellagio and Route 95.

Doug drove while Steve looked on his cell for information on the crash. The Las Vegas TV station K.L.V.H's website carried a detailed item datelined Creech Air Force Base, Nevada.

'Jemma, we may be OK,' Steve shouted from the back seat, straining to read the screen as the cell juddered in his hand in back of the tiny hatchback.

'Jesus, can't you stop bouncing this thing around? The goddam touch screen... There's a story here that talks about survivors including a member of the flight crew. He says they experienced a rapid loss of pressure at about twenty thousand feet while they were still climbing. The pilot had to make a sudden maneuver at about twelve thousand feet to avoid what looked like a light aircraft. The loss of cabin pressure resulted in the plane straying over Nellis Air Force base but eventually it came down at Creech. "The pilot made a heroic emergency landing in the desert"...

'... Here it is. At least 40 passengers and crew were rescued despite the aircraft catching fire after landing. Forty. Passengers and crew. That is nothing short of a miracle. Southwest Airlines has grounded its fleet of Boeing seven-thirty-sevens for inspection. O.K. This is fantastic. There will be some kind of support center at the base that can tell us where they are if they have been found.'

As he spoke, the needle touched eighty-five miles an hour as the vehicle sped along the highway but Jemma felt her mind brake to a crawl. Steve saved the story to his phone just as the signal broke.

The Stars and Stripes fluttered from the pole outside the U.S. Post Office in Indian Springs. The neat, cream-painted building, with its pink-tiled roof, had become the center of what could have passed for a fair, seen from the air. Its car park was filled with vehicles bearing the decals and badges of F.E.M.A. and the Clark County police and fire fighters and, incongruously, the Department of Public Works. The neighboring rough patch of land had been commandeered for hastily off-loaded cabins, to create a canteen and rest facilities for responders. T.V. crews had parked their R.V.s and trucks along the side of the highway, down the side road and alongside the cabins, while opposite, behind a wire fence, white vans and buses, and a solitary Jeep sat parked outside the low gray buildings at the edge of the air base as if nothing untoward had taken place. Steve slowed as the sparse settlement came into view and he spotted a roadblock manned by a Nevada Highway Patrol Trooper. When the trooper heard why they were there, he directed them to the Sheriff's office, which involved a U-turn and driving down a side road.

It was strangely quiet for the hub of operations. Newly elected Sheriff Zane Jameson, a handsome man with immaculate silver hair and crisp uniform, greeted them as if they had stopped in to leave a pie for one of his deputies. 'Coffee?' he beamed.

'No. Thank you,' said Jemma, slightly fazed. 'My fiancé and another friend were on board the crashed plane. We need to know if they are safe and we need to see them.'

'If you show deputy Alvirez your I.D. and the details of the persons you need to trace, he will look see if they are listed,' said the Sheriff. 'As you know, a passenger plane from McCarran International forced-landed inside the base. We have no jurisdiction there but we are coordinating with the military authorities and they are providing us with information. We have high-speed Internet but it's a bit slow right now. He will get this done for you as fast as he can.'

Alvirez took their I.D. and wrote down Mike and Gary's details including any distinguishing features, and went into a back office. The three could hear impressively fast typing and a series of questions asked sotto voce. After a wait of a minute or two, they heard him start up again, then he came back into the lobby. 'Neither name came up. They are not listed as deceased and if they are being treated they have not been identified.'

'Where are the injured being treated?' asked Jemma. 'Can we check to see if they are there? Maybe they have lost their I.D. or they can't communicate. We could identify them.'

The Sheriff replied, 'there is a field hospital on the air base with surgical facilities and they are caring for the walking wounded. They will have been triaged when they were rescued and some will have been dispersed to hospitals with E.R. in Las Vegas. I can give you a list.' He handed them a piece of paper. 'The rescue and clean-up operations are still in progress. They are still searching the area for survivors.'

'But what about people who are unhurt?' asked Steve. 'Where are they being taken?'

'We are contacting relatives of anyone who is leaving the air base and requests it,' said the Sheriff. 'I can assure you everything that can be done to locate, treat or account for survivors is being done and they are in good hands.'

'Can't we get on to the base to see if they are O.K?' asked Jemma.

'No unauthorized personnel are allowed on the installation,' the Sheriff smiled again. 'In the interests of national security.'

'But this is different. They have to make an exception.'

'I am sorry but the military's priority is security. We cannot rule out terrorist action here.'

'Can I call them?'

'We have a direct line and computer communications but they are restricted to state and local authorities. You would have to get clearance.'

'But this is crazy. My fiancée is in there.'

'I hope so, ma'am. I can only give you the information that I have. My advice is to find somewhere to stay and wait. Take my card. Leave a number where you're staying and we will contact you when we have news,' said the Sheriff. 'I am sorry to say the motel has been demolished along with the casino. There's a bed and breakfast but I would guess it's full. Your best bet is Las Vegas.'

'Can't we just explain to them?' asked Jemma.

'Call us,' purred the Sheriff, opening the door for them.

As they went back to the car, Steve could see Jemma was not about to sit meekly by the phone in Las Vegas or anywhere else.

'What just happened there?' asked Steve. 'Was that the run-around?'

'Do you still have that story on your phone?' asked Doug.

Steve took out the cell and found the story. It was

by-lined Brandy Knudsen. 'Give me a few minutes,' said Doug and headed towards the media encampment. Reporters and technicians stood drinking coffee, smoking or talking. He found a van signed K.L.V.H. by the highway, with its pneumatic satellite antennae raised about four feet, like the conning tower of a battle ship and coiled about with heavy cable. That was for point-to-point terrestrial and digital satellite transmission. There was also a low dome that Doug guessed covered a satellite phone antennae. By comparison to some of the beasts around there it was a relatively modest vehicle but it was built to get to places quickly and for filing multimedia stories. Better the low data rates of a satellite phone than no signal at all from Verizon, AT&T or the other mobile networks. It also had the advantage that the signal would be encrypted, so there was less chance of stories being intercepted. The van had an operating section up front and equipment storage, generator and cable reels in rear. It was locked up and apparently shut down, but he had an idea the Amazon with the red puffer jacket standing a ways off could be the person he was looking for. She might have a journalism major from Backwater College, he thought, but he doubted that was why she had been put in front of a camera. Her cheek bones, jaw, shoulders, breasts, hips: the whole woman jutted. Statuesque but doubtless as dense as marble, thought Doug.

'Brandy Knudsen. K.L.A.H.T.V?' he asked.

'That's me,' she said with a flash of expensive dentistry.

'Doug Reeder. W.G.B.H, out of Boston. I saw your piece on the web. Very good. Very detailed, particularly this early.'

'Why, thank you.'

'Two of my friends were on board and I have one their's fiancée with me here and desperate to find out what happened. I am guessing you had a heads-up from someone inside the air base, is that right?'

'You gotta get your own story, buddy,' said Brandy, cooling.

'Steady. I don't want to steal your story. I want a trade. I've done a lot of research on plane crashes'

'O.K.' she relented, cautiously. 'I would like to interview the fiancée.'

'I'll ask her. I can feed you technical information and put you in contact with experts but I need to get information from the other side of the wire.'

'They won't let you talk to anyone but the press liaison.'

'That would do.'

'You want to.use the sat phone, right?'

'I figured you'd have to have one. Yes. To call over there,' he said pointing the few yards to the fence.

'Sure. But I have one question.'

'Fire away.'

'Are you connected to the Douglas Reeder?'

'I am. He was my grandfather.'

'Wow. He's up there with Walter Kronkite and Ed Murrow. I did a term paper on him at Columbia.'

'You don't say,' said Doug, chastened.

She looked closer. He shared features with her old hero: the same dark curls, the thick cheeks, the heavy brows. He had dark rimmed glasses and behind them eyes that were as liable to sparkle as to glint, she noted.

'Sure. I always wondered what finally happened to him. Where he went.'

'I can't enlighten you on that. Maybe some time, when this is over?'

She gave him the number of the 432nd Wing Public Affairs mission, where he spoke to a Captain Briggs who told him to email a request and his press credentials. Brandy opened up a laptop in the van, keyed in a double password and he sent it over. He waited for four minutes to let the message girdle the globe and then called again.

'Captain Briggs is unavailable at present but you can receive updates on the current situation online, sir,' said a clerk. 'You have been emailed the website address.'

'Thanks Brandy,' said Doug. 'I am going to have to try something else but I'll get back you about Jemma'. He wrote down Mike and Gary's names on the back if his card and gave it to her. 'If you hear anything about these guys, please call.'

'Here's the sat phone number,' she said. 'Don't forget you owe me an interview.'

'Any luck?' asked Steve, when Doug got back. Doug shook his head.

'As soon as we can get a signal we need to start phoning the Las Vegas hospitals,' said Steve, pulling open the door to the Kia.

As they drove back to Las Vegas, they began to get bars on their phones. Doug searched for hospital numbers and scrawled them awkwardly in a notebook pressed against his knee. He called out the first number and Jemma dialed it on hers. The hospital had received emergency patients from the Creech air crash. They had been medevaced there within the last hour. But they could not be identified and anyways, patient details could not be given over the line. As they sped down Route 95 again, Jemma and Doug called the other hospitals. Five had received patients. In one, they were all female, two of them children.

'Dawn Hill has received eight patients from Creech. It has a trauma facility and it's the nearest. Head down town.' Doug shouted to Steve.

'Go, go. I'll find you,' said Doug as they drew up outside Dawn Hill. Steve and Jemma ran into the hospital. Doug found a parking spot and scrolled through the directory on his cell for Donny, an aviation medical examiner he had interviewed a year back.

'What are their chances?' he asked.

'You want it straight? How big are they and were they traveling coach or business?'

'One is about five, six and two hundred pounds. The other is about five foot ten inches and one-sixty pounds. They were traveling business.'

'Business is good. The height: not so good. Did the craft catch fire?'

'I don't know,' said Doug trying to recall the exact wording of the story. 'There was a plume of smoke but I think it was after the crash. I got the impression people may have got out before it went up.'

'O.K. If it wasn't a fireball it could just have been an oil fire. That's good. Let's put that to one side. They would have a better chance up front anyway. In general, head injuries are the most common, followed by multiple blunt injuries, fractures and chest injuries. If the tall one is long-limbed he may have broken his leg or suffered amputation. Without knowing anything about the crash itself, whether the airplane rolled, the type and location of structural damage, what kind of terrain it was in…'

'Desert. And there was some kind of rip in the fuselage.'

'O.K. So there was probably decompression. You don't have long to get your oxygen mask on but assuming they got through that O.K. there's the impact. You get hit with the chair in front or the armrest. Cabin furniture and luggage bins detach and fly forward. It's not good. There is high risk of injury to the ribs, face, lungs and liver. The brain and eyes are commonly avulsed.'

'Avulsed?'

'Forcibly detached.'

'Oh, Jesus.'

'Is this distressing you?'

'No. No. Keep going.'

'O.K,' said Donny, warming to his subject, 'So: It's a curious feature of this type of accident that decapitation tends to happen above the maxilla – at the top of the head -- rather than the neck – as you might expect… But that's the worst-case scenario. People can walk away from a crash.'

'If the worst has happened and Gary and Mike are dead, when will we know?'

'It depends if they have documentation on them. A forensic pathologist will go through documents, fingerprints, dental records, personal effects and D.N.A. of course. It's obviously easier and quicker with whole bodies. Fragments are sorted by body part, size, the extent of burns and so on. You really want to know all this?'

'Yes. I need to know.'

'If you don't find out within the next day or so, you should know within a month at the max. That's if they are dead. One or both could be fine.'

'Donny, mind if I pass your name on to a reporter?'

'Sure.'

Doug found Jemma and Steve at the E.R. desk where they had spoke to an admissions clerk with a portable computer. She had just returned from collecting the details of the most recent admissions including the patients from Creech. She checked the screen. 'I can't tell you who is in there,' she said,' but I can tell you your husband is not one of them. There is no Michael or Roland in there and no one named Gary or Cohan.'

'No John Does?' asked Jemma.

'Only a guy who was stabbed in a fight and he is seventy years old.'

Jemma and Steve checked the other hospitals, each time drawing a blank and not knowing whether that was good or bad news. Jemma could feel herself wearing down. Doug, meantime, had phoned the Indian Springs Sheriff's office three times and had received the same patient and polite reply on each try. Then he called the Public Affairs mission at Creech and was given the same story as before. Doug's gut told him they were being stonewalled.

Steve's phone rang. He saw it was Becca calling. 'Oh crap. We should have called her,' he said moving away. Without even listening to his half of the conversation the other two could tell it was bad news: Gary was dead.

'The airline informed her as next of kin. She didn't know he was with Mike. She just wanted to talk to someone who knew him. They will have to do an autopsy.' The others had already gathered as much.

'Poor bastard,' said Steve glumly. 'Poor crazy bitch.'

Jemma went to the washroom, locked herself into a stall and wept.

'It's not looking good, is it?' said Steve, dropping his voice. 'I don't know if you gathered but there is already some kind of conspiracy shit up on the web about the crash.'

'Terrorists?'

'Aliens, would you believe? Becca heard about Gary an hour ago and went on some forum. They are saying it was brought down by an alien spacecraft, for crying out loud. What is wrong with these people?' Steve sighed. 'Do we start over here or do we go back to Indian Springs?'

'I've got a real feeling Mike is O.K. And I have an idea who can help us find him. But we'll need gas,' said Doug.

Chapter Six

The Deal

Palm Springs, CA. 1954

James Haggerty had a different way with the press. Truman's man Short was like Truman: if he trusted you, you were in. If you were in, you were in; if you were out, you were out. Haggerty thought he was a lot smarter than he was.

Truman's popularity had collapsed as he ran a war overseas and battled with both houses over the race issue and what-all. Ike chose to run with the Republicans but he could have been President by public acclaim, an elected king. "I like Ike" worked for the campaign and the charm had not worn off. The day Ike's motorcade rolled into Palm Springs, more than two thousand people were out to greet him and Mamie. For a week Paul Helms's second home, The Smoke Tree Ranch, would be the Western White House and the press were put up at the El Mirador. With its fake Spanish Colonial bell tower, Olympic-sized pool, tennis courts and stables, it was hardly a motel. While their colleagues were off chasing stories about Soviet spy cells and commies in Michigan, the press boys inside Haggerty's gilded cage slipped into a state of torpor.

Having dragged around after the President on his quail-hunting vacation just a week earlier in Georgia, the Chicago Tribune's Laurence Burd phoned over a rather peevish non-story for the February 20th edition. A copy editor picked up its tone of frustration. Page three, column one was headlined, 'Ike tackles his mail then he's off to the golf course.' The stand-first read: 'He bars reporters from even a glimpse.' Ike had, in fact, granted the press a shot of himself putting and posing over the hole with Helms and a few others. Haggerty had even fixed it so they included Ben Hogan, the golf pro, but why let the facts get in the way?

The more pliant members of the press were left to their own devices at the El Mirador while the 'bad sports', whose core were Burd, Douglas Reeder from I.N.S, and Lyle Johnson from A.P., were diverted with a barbecue on the other side of town and plied with drink.

Ike's game at the at the Tamarisk Country Club had been a sham and as soon as Heggarty had shepherded the photographers away Ike's official friends made themselves scarce and he was taken to the Smoke Tree Ranch. Beetle Smith ushered him in to meet the hastily convened handful of men about to recast the future of mankind. He was still dressed in a check shirt and sweater. Smith was ostensibly there as head of the C.I.A., since Majestic's existence was unknown to the others: Lieutenant Colonel Philip Corso had recently joined the National Security Council and could give a Pentagon and intelligence perspective. Earl Warren, the new Chief Justice of the United States was there to give a view on the constitution. Edwin Nourse, the chairman of the Council of Economic Advisors, would advise on finance. Cardinal James Francis MacIntyre the Cardinal of the Western United States would provide a moral compass, and the 80-year old Franklin Winthrop Allen, formerly of the Hearst Newspapers Group, would know how to handle public opinion. Not one smiled.

'Gentlemen. Thank you for attending at short notice,' Ike began. 'I believe General Smith has apprised you of the situation. It is unprecedented and urgent. We are about to enter talks with an alien race whose abilities and intentions we cannot truly comprehend and whose existence flies in the face of everything we have been taught. You have had very little time to come to terms with the facts, the reality. They are here and they are ready to talk.'

It was extraordinary how ordinary mean could cope with their fear, thought Eisenhower. Even he, used as he was to briefings loaded with foreknowledge of suffering in the abstract, even he marveled at their coolness, their academic, cold-blooded calm.

I would not risk one soldier's life by putting these men into battle alongside them, he thought, and yet here they are, focused, rational and willing to lend their minds, their experience to a situation graver than anything a sane person would expect to encounter in their entire lives. Here am I, about to make the single most important, the most vital meeting in mankind's history, with creatures I know nothing about, whose powers I can only pray are constrained and their actions governed by some code better than our own. How much destruction and cruelty have we witnessed for all our so-called civilization? The millennia of barbarity, the unending, tangled trail of blood and tears. What horrors might their longer history contain? How many times our own tally of crusades, of crucifixions, what multiple of billions of acts of inhumanity. Generation on generation, from the Fall. Here we are, the word genocide barely coined, still shaking from total war, terrified the Reds will someday blast us to hell and yet here too are these men. Detached. Analytical. Their very equanimity bore in on him the unease he had had as a commander without combat experience. If he were a lone soldier preparing to face an enemy with unimaginable superiority, they were the generals way back behind the lines. Safe, warm, well fed and remote. He felt an iron collar round his throat.

'You are each experts in your field. General Smith, Colonel Corso and myself are simple soldiers but we know the importance of strategy,' he told them. 'None of us likes surprises, particularly when they are sprung by, let's say, a force whose disposition and strength we cannot measure.

The unknown. The unknowable. The collar tightened.

'General Smith will have told you that since we have been monitoring the presence of these aliens there has been no sign of a threat from them. Even so, we cannot assume they are benign or that that they are here to advance our interests over theirs, any more than we can assume that they are preparing some kind of attack or domination. We do not know whether we can trust them but we can be clear that it must be better to have an understanding, an agreement, with them than the uncertainty that spurning their approach would involve.

'They initiated this and, as you now know, General Smith has been acting as liaison, our emissary, if you like. We are scheduled to meet at a military location a short distance from here. We shall not be entering these discussions completely blind or unarmed but it is imperative that we leave them knowing that whatever we plan, or have agreed, is in the interests of the United States of America and the world.' Ike folded his hands and looked to Smith.

'We do not have a great deal of time, so if you could be brief,' said Smith to the advisors.

Earl Warren cleared his throat. 'None of the laws of the United States of America nor any other jurisdiction were framed with this sort of situation in mind.'

'Are you saying the President will be acting illegally if he signs a treaty?' asked Smith.

'If you will allow me to continue,' Warren replied, 'the principle issue is that treaties are formed between nations. The nations of the Earth. It could be argued that any group that is extraterrestrial must ipso facto be non-national. On the other hand, new nations can be brought into existence. Until they are, they too are non-nations or non-states. They become nations or states by merit of being recognized as such.'

'We do not have the luxury of discussing this with

the State Department or the Senate. Can the President alone recognize them and enter a treaty with them?' asked Eisenhower.

'Under clause two, section two of the United States Constitution, a treaty would have to receive the approval of two-thirds of the senate. But in the United States versus Belmont in 1937 the Supreme Court upheld the power of the President to sign an executive agreement recognizing the Soviet Union and to establish diplomatic relations without consulting the Senate,' said Warren. 'My personal judgment is that that would allow you to do the same, today, with these non-terrestrials.'

Eisenhower nodded and turned to Nourse.

'There is no point in sugar-coating it,' said Nourse. 'The economy is in downturn. It has suffered from a three quarter recession and we face the prospect of output falling this year. You need to get some kind of deal that gets us out of this mess or any prospect of a tax cut for Middle America will evaporate.'

Winthrop Allen gave Nourse a look of deep disdain. You have got to be kidding, he thought. A tax cut for Middle America? Had Nourse really understood what was being discussed? However you framed it, an economist was a hoo-doo man. He might as well be reading the cards. But if economics were a well-paid form of magic act, the uncertainties and assumptions it involved were as nothing compared to dealing with an alien form of life that might be as different to men as clouds were to rocks. We might as well try to communicate with a virus or a god.

'I see,' Eisenhower, said to Nourse. 'Your eminence?'

'I wonder why you are asking me. You are not one of our flock, are you Mister President? Indeed you are rarely to be found in any congregation.'

'No. I am not, Frank, but the Catholic Church reaches beyond our borders and what happens today will affect the whole of Creation.'

'The Holy Father has not spoken on this matter directly. However, in 'Humani Generis' his holiness spoke of evolution. The idea that there is such a process is not incompatible with our Christian faith which obliges us to hold that souls are immediately created by God. He is the creator. These, creatures, these beings, are his creatures too. They are sentient, so it is likely the Lord gave them souls and certain they will damn themselves if they do us harm. I cannot advise you further, my son, except to say that if these creatures are looking for allies it would be better that they were us than the Soviets.'

You guys have come a long way since Galileo, thought the old newspaperman. 'If I may venture a purely editorial opinion, Mister President,' he said, in an oak-aged rumble. 'This is the biggest story that can never be told. Any deal that you make with these beings will take us in a new and completely unpredictable direction: towards knowledge and wealth or enslavement in perpetuity. If the former, we must maintain our advantage. We saw what happened with the atomic bomb and how fast the Soviets were to close any lead that we had over them. Knowledge is power. If we alert the American public to this we also alert the Kremlin. If we come out of this badly, and we well might, constitutional niceties or the economy will be the least of our problems; we will face annihilation.'

'Colonel?'

'In my view, we should only ever negotiate from strength. The fact they have approached us suggests they are weak or need something. This is our planet. We need to show them who's boss.'

Ike invoked Pericles. 'I concur and in that respect, I have some reassuring news,' he said. 'Right now, on an atoll in the Marshall Islands, we are demonstrating a weapon that is many times more powerful even than the atomic bombs we have used and tested to date. I have ordered the explosion of this new dry fuel hydrogen bomb to be brought forward, ahead of our meeting with the E.B.E.s. While the test is taking place many thousands of miles from here and therefore should not be perceived as a direct threat to them, I believe these beings were attracted when we tested Trinity. They are aware of our power but are fearful of it and they will very shortly realize that it is increasing with time. This will strengthen our hand.' He looked each in the eye, in turn. 'Thank you all for your advice.' The iron collar loosened.

The cardinal leant forward and said, in an almost conspiratorial whisper, 'Mister President, take courage. The battle is not yours but God's. Da pacem, Domine, in diebus nostris.'

Burd, Reeder and Johnson had made a break from Heggarty's barbecue and returned to the El Mirador, smashed. The trio had hatched a half-brained plan to take a horse each and ride over to the Smoke Tree Ranch, with the idea of bearding Ike in his den. When they got there, though, Heggarty had headed them off. He fed them a line about Ike having chipped a tooth and having been taken off to a dentist. He was a manipulative bastard but he could not lie to save his life. So, the three amigos rode back to the El Mirador where, despite the efforts of the two more mature men, Johnson picked up a phone and called in a story that the President was dead from a heart attack. It was a career move of the wrong kind, but not as big a mistake as missing the real deal, the scoop of all time. Reeder woke with a sick feeling that was more than dyspepsia. His reporter's gut was churning.

The journey by road from Palm Springs to Edwards A.F.B. would have taken more than two and a half hours, maybe three, so Smith had arranged for a Piper Pacer to land out back of the Ranch to cut the time in half. 'Columbine', the presidential Lockheed Constellation, remained on Palm Springs Air Field. Aboard the Piper there was room for the pilot, the President, Smith, and Floyd Boring, who was armed with a Colt 1903 and a borrowed Police Thompson gun with a 30-round magazine. There was a tailwind and they made good time flying up the Yucca Valley and over Victorville.

The short flight gave Ike time to ruminate. Waiting were representatives of an alien culture whose technology enabled them to travel incalculable distances by unfathomable means. No one could know what knowledge, what materials, what power they might have under their control. Were they here to teach, to dominate or for some other purpose? With no idea of their customs or their capabilities this could be the only chance he, Ike, would have to speak with them for humanity or it could be the first of many meetings, a dialogue of two worlds.

The way he figured it, evolution was about survival and that would apply wherever they came from. They needed to survive. And whatever they were after, to get it they had had to develop amazing technology, perhaps taking generations to do so, and then apply it to searching the whole of the Milky Way, star by star, to find ours. There had to be a point to their being here even if the logic it was reached by was alien. If they had something to lose we had something to gain. Was this the first exchange in diplomacy, the first recon in a war or the first move in a game, a game with unimagined stakes and an unimaginable pot?

He knew the utter necessity of intelligence. Other

than the little Smith had shared and the counsel of the remaining Majestic 12, there was none to be had. All anyone really knew about these creatures was that they were here. They undoubtedly knew far more about us. He wondered if that sighting on the radio bridge of the F.D.R. had been luck or something more.

Smith had had a prototype two-band VHF receiver hastily installed in the Piper and he called ahead to Edwards for a cleared landing. As soon as the plane put down, the three passengers transferred to a Jeep and were taken to the meeting place, a cabin alongside a hangar guarded by Air Police. An ambulance stood by.

Boring instinctively braced, ready to fire the Tommy gun, as he surveyed the interior of the hangar. Inside was a large silver craft: a flying saucer. It was featureless with a completely smooth dull-silver casing, but no wings or engines. Anxious lest it distract him, Boring inspected every space and shadow. Curiosity was tugging Ike towards the craft but he clung to the doorway like Odysseus strapped to the mast. Smith misread the awe and fascination the advanced technology inspired in Ike and reassured him that the area had been swept with Geiger counters by the Army Chemical Corps. Air samples had been taken, he whispered. As far as they could tell there was no contamination from radiation or germs. 'How would they know? The Aztecs had no idea what smallpox was,' said Ike.

Just then, Lieutenant colonel Corso arrived by Jeep.

In war, Ike liked his odds short: his risks low, his rewards high. He liked to throw up a smoke screen, occupy the high ground, send his men in with their backs to the sun. He had learned to play poker back in Abiline from a fellow called Bob Davis. Bob could barely write his own name but he could read a man. Ike skinned his classmates at West Point. These days he played Bridge but he had not forgotten how to take low and still come out on top. And he knew the bank always wins. If he was about to participate in a game with no idea what cards his opponents held, the rules they played by or their aim, he had to be the dealer. Assuming their communications were as good as their transportation, they would know that humans, Americans, had just exploded a massive weapon over a chain of remote islands in the Pacific. Their kind might even have seen it from outer space, a human-made sun on the face of our blue planet. He might have no idea how they were armed or how many of them there were but at least he would have a gun to lay on the table and it would be smoking.

'Have we had a report yet on Castle Bravo?' he demanded.

'The test over Bikini atoll has been delayed,' Corso said hurriedly. 'There is a problem with the bomb.'

This was a disaster. For a split second the world went black.

'How long a delay?' the President growled.

He had been disarmed. He would be meeting these creatures like a lone, dumb child. Like a turtle with its shell torn off.

'Days. Possibly weeks. They are worried about the fusion fuel. They believe they may have underestimated the yield.'

'All the more reason to test it,' growled Ike. 'Damn Oppenheimer.'

His mouth dried. His palms sweated. There was nothing left to do but bluff. He waited to bring his breathing and his heart rate under control as he prepared to enter the building. He was about to step into an abyss, hauling the whole of humanity. Nothing in life, nothing on Earth had prepared this leader of the Free World, this singular representative of his people – of all people – for the coming encounter and its consequences. What was that line from Shakespeare? 'As flies to wanton schoolboys are we to the gods.' Lear. The impotent, foolish old man.

Smith had briefed Ike on what to expect of the E.B.Es, at least physically. There were just two of them. They were repulsive. Although they had two arms and two legs like a human and stood upright they had disturbingly smooth skin, not like a porpoise's, more like a slug's and battle ship gray. They had squat, pot-bellied bodies. The head was pear-shaped with a bulbous cranium and a small chin beneath a narrow slit, which Ike took to be a mouth, and two smaller slits above that for nostrils. He could not tell if they had ears or not. But their eyes were bug-like, bigger than a human's and black like shiny buttons. Smith had commandeered some bulbs from the control tower and the room was under red light; apparently they had trouble with sunlight. Their lack of expression was disconcerting. Their movements were languid. Both wore featureless uniforms, whose surfaces had a viscous appearance. The fabric stretched over their plump pygmy bodies from neck to ground and incorporated their large feet so that they didn't need boots. Their breathing was audible, like that of a child whose nasal passages are full of mucus. They didn't appear to speak to one another but they used a device to communicate with him. Perhaps they also spoke to each other using telepathy. They moved their thumbless hands over an object that resembled a glass tray and from somewhere in its vicinity came a flat, buzzy voice that spoke in English. It took a moment to realize that real words were coming from it. They sounded like someone un-practised reading from a script – over the airplane's radio. Nevertheless, it was English. 'Are you the leader?' it asked.

With Smith at his side, Ike began asking questions that would enable them both to know whether this was little more than an intergalactic courtesy call or the aliens were delivering the terms of a surrender. It soon became clear that neither was the case. Instead, these creatures were, they said, on a mercantile mission: they were traders. Before Ike had gotten very far, the disembodied voice from the E.B.Es' gadget had laid out a simple bargain. The aliens were a long way from home. They would trade advanced technology for the fuel and materials they needed to continue their journey. Ike elicited a promise that they were not intent on harming our species, directly through conflict or by another means. They agreed.

Both sides had conditions for the trade: Ike wanted another assurance that they would not interfere in human affairs; the aliens wanted a small base, an entrepot, from which they could operate unhindered. 'That can be arranged,' said the President.

'We wish to learn about your planet,' said the voice.

'We too wish to learn about and from you,' said Ike. 'We will make an agreement.'

'It is agreed,' said the voice.

So there it was. In less than half an hour the course of human history had been altered completely, irrevocably and in complete secret. Why, it took longer to explain that the need for a written treaty and longer still to arrange for it to be formalized by representatives of both species. Ike had arrived empty-handed and appeared to be leaving with the promise of a new age for mankind. He was in a daze. He knew though, that he had just participated in the single most important event in human history. He and Smith and the nameless alien creatures. Even if the details, the timetable, the process, the manpower, the costs, or the nature of the technology on offer had yet to be put in place, Ike had a deal and it included the safety of the human race and peace for our time. Too bad, humanity must never know.

Chapter Seven

Holding pattern

Soleded Springs, NV. Present.

Bob Tilson's shiny trailer was easy to spot in back of the Space Station. Doug remembered the array of antennae and domes along its roof. As he, Steve and Jemma approached, Tilson bounded out of the vehicle with his finger to his lips, indicating silence. 'Inside. Heads down,' he said. He made a fist, with his thumb and pinky out to mimick making a call, and collected their phones. As they entered, he pointed to the icebox, opened it and put their cells inside. They clambered into a space with a table littered with a pile of box files heaped next to an old Olivetti portable typewriter and a laptop computer.

'So you're back,' he grinned. It was as if they were old friends – more than brief, bar acquaintances, but buddies from way back.

Doug nodded. 'We're looking for our friend Mike. He and Gary were on that plane that came down. Gary died. Mike is missing…'

'But not presumed dead,' said Bob.

Yes. I guess,' said Doug, not missing a beat. He turned and indicated Jemma. 'This is Jemma, Mike's partner. We think there is a chance that Mike survived but we can't get any information.'

'Steve and Doug think you know more about that place than you told them about when you all met,' said Jemma. 'Can you help us?'

'You bet,' said Bob. 'But you're going to have to understand some pretty weird shit before we take the next step. Stuff you're going think is whacky, like I am off my head.' He looked from face to face, then back to Jemma. 'You ready?'

Bob opened a cupboard lined with more box files held in place with a strap, and replaced the ones he had been consulting. He unrolled a map that had various notes written neatly on to it and areas shaded with colored marker. 'This here is a map of the Nellis Ranges. This is Area 51, Groom and Area 52, Papoose also called Area 54 or S-4 for 'Satellite four'. The actual lake is here over the mountain range behind Groom Lake and South of Area 51, which you have probably heard of. This is Frenchman Lake. Here: Pehute Mesa. And Dog Bone Lake, running north to south on Range 62.

'If you look at a regular map or look on the web you will not see what is on here because it's all classified. More secret than Top Secret. Their very existence has been classed as Sensitive Compartmented Information for half a century. Your partner's flight came down in an area that is next to a no-go area where even most of the military are refused access. If your partner is alive and he is in there but they are not telling you he may be here,' said Bob, stabbing a point on the neck of a large bottle-shaped area, with his finger.

'That would be better news than him being here,' he said pointing to the northwest corner. 'If he has gotten into that area, there would be no chance of retrieving him. It would be like tracking down and rescuing a P.O.W. in North Korea. Tougher. And it's nothing to do with nuclear. Nuclear is everyday stuff to those boys. If you were a V.I.P. you could book a tour of the nuclear facilities and the firing ranges and they would probably throw in a drone display for good measure. Hell, at least nine countries have nuclear arsenals and, if you don't mind the Feds watching you for the rest of your life, you just have to click your mouse to find out how you make a bomb.'

Doug broke in. 'We were given the brush-off by the sheriff's office and why is Mike not in any of the hospitals in Las Vegas? I tried going through the Air Force media liaison but I know when I am being blocked.'

'If Mike is in there, how would you know?' asked Jemma.

'Jemma Ellen deSilva. Born August first, 1985. Mother: Portuguese Indian. Father: American. Your were educated at the English School, Boston, Massachusetts and Brown University, Rhode Island, where you majored in Computer Science and that is where you met Michael Alan Roland who was over from Cambridge University, England. You are currently working as an independent consultant. You do not possess a driver's license and you have no criminal record.' Bob grinned. 'Leonard Nimoy went to your school. Did you know that?'

Steve's eyes narrowed. 'What is going on here? We tell you someone survived a major air disaster and he is out there. And you don't bat an eye and then you come up with this?' Bob smirked. Steve could feel his gorge rising. 'I don't buy that this is some spooky desert intuition,' he said. 'This is one dumb, cheap trick. You just did that then, didn't you? Jemma's age and education are on her Linkedin profile. Not the other records you checked those too.'

'No. I had someone else do it,' said Bob. 'I saw you arrive and guessed who you were. I use The Onion Ring – that's a browser you can't snoop on, for the rest of you guys. They probably know you're here anyway but it helps.'

'And what have "they" got to do with Mike and how we find him?' asked Doug.

'You have to understand that what I am about to tell you will sound a little crazy, a lot crazy. But I swear it's true. All governments, by their nature are disinclined to communicate honestly with their citizens. They all try to manage the message. The decent politicians are too busy to explain what they are doing the whole time. The other guys just lie. You can have the C.I.A. on top of one hill in a conflict and Military Intelligence on top of another and they won't talk to each other because they don't trust each other to keep whatever secret they've got, which is probably the same secret. Or no secret. What I am saying is organizations have a natural tendency to protect themselves. The military: even more so. Sometimes they are genuinely doing it for our own good and sometimes for their own operational convenience. Anything that could loosely be termed national security gives them a reason to hold back. Their job is to protect us and sometimes that means they have to keep secrets. All O.K. so far?'

'Bob. We are not kids,' said Jemma.

'Sometimes people keep secrets because they are embarrassed. We have all done that. Big organizations do it when they have really messed up and they have poisoned half a city to save a few lousy cents on some safety measure. Or they have been caught bugging the Watergate. You get the idea. So in the arena of the military industrial complex, which is what we are talking about here, there are some secrets that only people with security clearance are allowed to know. There are also some secrets that are further restricted to a small group directly accountable to the head of a department or organization. In theory, they are all ultimately accountable to the President, and, he is accountable to the people. Hooray for the red, white and blue. Except there are some secrets that are too big even for the President to know. And one of them is right here.'

'And you know this, how?' Doug demanded.

'Sources.'

'Sources? Hmm…'

'So if he is alive, Mike is somewhere in a top secret site and we cannot find out because?... '

'Because he knows something, and they don't know what it is, or how serious it is. And as long as they don't know they will hold on to him so they can find out because, ironically, they don't like secrets either.'

Jemma's eyes widened. 'And if he doesn't know anything, which he probably doesn't. What then?'

'They will think he does but that he's holding out.'

'And if they find something?'

'Then they have to keep it a secret.'

'You mean kill him?' she said.

'No. Not necessarily,' said Bob hurriedly. 'They have other means. And now that you have put yourself on their radar, you have the potential to be a real pain in the ass for them. If you haven't heard to the contrary within a matter of days, he's alive and they are holding him.'

Doug said: 'People can be hard to identify and not because they are injured but just because they don't have papers. Maybe they just don't know who he is.'

'They are going to want everyone accounted for, processed or bagged and tagged and off their land, so they become someone else's problem,' Bob replied. 'Ordinarily, it would be in their interests to cooperate but not if he knows something, or they think he does.'

Doug tried to break the spell. 'Bob. Who are "they"?'

'There is a secret parallel government. Mike's plane was brought down by one of its craft,' said Bob. 'An alien space craft.'

Steve saw red. 'You cannot be serious,' he blurted. 'Are you kidding us with this paranoid, conspiracy bullshit? We drive into the middle of nowhere to indulge your fantasies. Now? Right now? You freak!' Steve's eyes blazed like lasers. 'And Doug: you're a total idiot, too, for dragging us out here.'

Jemma put her hand on the top of Steve's arm. 'It's OK. It's OK,' she said. 'Doug. I think we had better go.'

Mike woke.

The room was plain and bare. Just the cot Mike lay on and one chair for furniture. The drapes were closed.

Mike's head felt heavy on the clean crisp pillow. The sheet was drawn neatly across his chest and his arms were outside it, straight at his sides.

'A man in a white coat, stocky, bullet-headed with sallow skin, took a pen flashlight and shone it into Mike's eyes. 'Look up. Down, Left. Right,' said the man. Mike complied automatically.

'Good,' said the man in white. 'How do you feel?'

'A little giddy. A little nauseous. My legs ache.'

'OK. We can fix that. Now, I am going to ask you some questions and …'

'Why am I here? What has happened?'

'You were in an accident and you were hurt but you are mending now.'

'What sort of accident?'

'The serious kind. Your legs ache because you broke them quite badly and you had internal injuries. You lost part of your spleen. You damaged your arm, as well.'

Mike's hand went to this side. It ached. His legs ached, too, but they weren't in plaster and they appeared to be whole. 'How is your head?' You had a piece of metal removed from your skull. A small plastic plate has replaced the bone there.'

'How long have I…?'

'Do you remember what happened?'

Mike shook his head.

'What is the last thing you recall?'

'I was at my desk. I was looking at a paper on phyllotaxis, the numerology of plants.'

'Do you know why?'

'A conference. I had been to a conference or I was going to one.'

'What else do you remember?'

'It was on Lucas numbers and patterns in nature. I can't remember the detail.'

'Anything else.'

Mike shook his head.

'Sure?'

Mike frowned, searching.

'How do you feel now?'

'Tired.'

'Get some sleep. I'll look in on you later.'

'What we have here is a U.S.A.F. abbreviated accident investigation report on a mishap with a Predator drone near Creech Air Force Base on the day Mike and Gary's flight crashed,' said Bob, opening a folder and carefully placing the document on the table, next to his typewriter. 'This does not prove that they still have Mike but it does show that they are hiding something big.'

Doug took a sip of his coffee. He was better off meeting Bob on his own.

'At 1008 Zulu time and MQ-1B remotely piloted aircraft…' Bob read, as he ran his finger over the document, '… at approximately 1008… I love that "approximately" 1008… a remotely piloted aircraft, herein referred to as the mishap R.P.A., tail number 01-4098, impacted the ground approximately 13 nautical miles north-east of Creech Air Force Base, Nevada four point five hours into a training mission. The M.R.P.A. and one M-36 training missile were destroyed on impact. The total damage to United States government property was estimated to be four point five million dollars. There was no other damage to government or civilian property.' He paused. 'It's a lie, of course.'

'They said Mike's flight was the result of a near miss with a light aircraft, not a drone,' said Doug.

‘Sure they did. That was a cover-up.’

‘Well what is this, then? This drone business?’

‘It’s a cover-up of the cover-up.’

‘You know I’m really starting to understand why Jemma had such severe doubts about you.’

‘This is how it works. You remember the Lockerbie bombing, over Scotland?’

‘Sure.’

‘There are still people who think al-Megrahi, the Libyan bomber, was set up.’

‘Was he?’

‘I have no idea. Probably. What I do know is that it won’t go away, even though the new governments in Libya want it to and so does the White House.’

‘So the light aircraft wasn’t real, but the drone was?

‘No. No. Keep up. The light aircraft did not cause the crash and neither did the drone but if you realized the light aircraft had not done it you would think they were covering up that some guy at a Playstation in Creech lost concentration and wrote off four million bucks. And. And – here is the clever part: they are saying it had nothing to do with the crash. Either people accept that it was not involved or they look for proof that it was. Either way the focus is at ninety degrees to the truth. At worst, they pay compensation in twenty years’ time when the so-called facts are locked into place. Except we will still know it was an alien scout craft.’

'You really believe that?'

'I do.'

'What if that's wrong, too? What if it's something else altogether?'

'Like what?'

'I have no idea but the black boxes would have something, particularly the audio. If the pilot saw something coming at them in mid-air he would sure as hell say so.'

'They can take months to process and that's long enough to fake evidence if they want to.'

Doug took a look out of the window at hills where Bob was convinced Mike was being held. Bob might be right about the whole light aircraft-drone deception but if he tried to use it as leverage to get information on Mike's whereabouts he would just get laughed at. 'We need something more concrete,' he said.

'If you wanted to wait for two months,' said Bob, 'all the autopsy material will have been processed, and the investigators should have made a preliminary report to the chain of command.' He cleaned his glasses on the corner of his shirt-front. 'They won't release it though.'

'Can't we find out what they already have? What about public interest?'

'In theory. But they decide what is in the public interest.' Bob opened a box file and riffled through the contents. 'Article 2254 of the U.S. Code,' he said, handing Doug a sheet of paper. 'Start where it says Public Disclosure.'

Doug read: 'The Secretary concerned, upon request, shall publicly disclose unclassified tapes, scientific reports, and other factual information pertinent to an aircraft accident investigation, before the release of the final accident investigation report relating to the accident.' He looked at Bob. 'Surely that's good isn't it?'

'First, he will only disclose unclassified material. And everything's classified. And second, look just below there. He only has to release it if it "would not compromise national security". Guess who defines that.'

When Mike woke again, it still appeared to be day. Had he only been out for a few minutes? He recalled the conversation he had had with the bullet-headed man in the white coat. Everything else was just out of reach. He could have been out for weeks or minutes. He could barely sit up but, with effort, he slowly began to swing himself off the bed and stand. His legs were unsteady and his balance was poor but he shuffled towards the window and tugged at the drapes. They opened to reveal a blank wall. Mike touched it gingerly to check that it was solid. With a mounting feeling of alarm he moved towards the door. It had a wired glass that looked on to a dimly lit, and featureless corridor. He pushed against the doorplate and felt the door move. It glided open so easily that he tottered forward.

The room was in the middle of the corridor. He could see now that the corridor was lined with similar rooms. He crossed over to the one opposite and peered through the glass. It was empty except for a bed and mattress with blue and white ticking and a single hard-backed chair. The corridor went for thirty yards in each direction and ended in a turn.

Mike turned and began moving slowly, and with some pain, towards the corner. Just as he reached it, he saw a darkening on the wall ahead, a faint shadow. He turned to go back but it was too late. A man in gray fatigues turned the corner and seeing Mike, reached for a large flat gun at his hip.

Mike could hear the Taser clicking like a roach as the man moved forward, one arm outstretched, the other aiming the weapon. The guard fired, jamming Mike's wasted muscles and scrambling his brain. Paralyzed and dazed, Mike slipped and cracked his head against the wall. His attacker lifted him under his arms and carried him back to his bed.

As he lay there alone, slumped awkwardly against the bed head, he could feel what little strength he had draining away but he forced himself to remain awake. And for a while he managed it, leaning on one elbow and straining to hear a noise, any noise from outside.

But then he must have dropped off because as he looked up he saw the man in white watching him.

Jemma was on the line to a member of the Redtail Air Victims Support Group, a stewardess called Corrine. Jemma knew she must have been asked again and again whether she remembered the person someone had lost and who was one of the 'lucky' ones. Corrine had acted superbly, bringing more than her training into helping passengers away from the smashed plane, going back time and again to bring them a safe distance. Perhaps that is why she was coping so much better than her colleague Beth-May, whom Jemma had also called only to find her vague and aggressive in turns. Corrine had at least been taken to a field hospital and treated for shock.

Corrine could not remember whether she had seen or helped Mike, although she thought she remembered Gary from the description of his red hair. She had been questioned numberless times about the passengers and the moments before the plane suddenly banked, before the grinding scream as the fuselage ripped itself open, the oxygen masks releasing like a swarm of jelly fish, before she saw a choking mother struggling to put a mask over her little boy's face. Before the press, before the emails, Corrine had come home to dozens of phone messages from colleagues and had calmly phoned them all back. She had tried to make sense of what happened. Planes don't just fall apart. There must have been a cause. She had heard the official story about a light aircraft and the scuttlebutt about a U.F.O. She had witnessed the optical illusion of a shape hovering and then zooming away on occasion, when she had looked out over the wing and through the cabin window. She guessed that was what people had seen, but she was beginning to doubt her memory. She fought off flashbacks and daymare scenarios, imagined arguments with flight control, the captain, suspicious passengers. The only thing she could do, she told Jemma, was to get back to work and fight her demons. If she remembered anything at all about Mike, she would let Jemma know. 'I have to find my way to closure. I hope you're right and I hope you find him. I truly do,' she said. 'But if you have lost him, I pray you find out for sure. Soon.'

Bob typed, 'the good news: My source confirms M's plane ran into an alien scout craft.'

'The bad news?'

'It was the tail of the scout craft'.

'So?'

'A.S.C.s don't have tails.'

'Maybe he was wrong?'

'Disinformation. We're getting the cover story now, when we should be getting the skinny. I shouldn't have trusted them.'

'Sure you're not just being paranoid?'

There was a sharp rap at the motel room door. Steve was there, accompanied by two men, one Jemma had never seen before and another she might have seen at some time but had no time to recall. 'They were at reception when I arrived,' Steve said.

The first of the two men showed a solid-looking badge like a Western marshal's and announced that he was from the U.S. Air Force Office of Special Investigations. He confirmed Jemma and Steve's identities and then began to question them. His name sounded like Fleck or Fletch. His voice was dull, mechanical, almost hypnotic.

'As you know ma'am, RedTail Flight 488 struck a military installation. It crashed in an area designated as a bombing range. It also an area where advanced weaponry is tested. That is not classified. Military aviation investigators have been carrying out a thorough examination of the crash site. All the wreckage has been collected and analyzed. The whole site has been examined inch by inch and every item collected, logged and analyzed. So far, all the passengers and crew have been accounted for, except your partner, Michael Alan Roland. There is no trace of his having been on board, except the records taken at check-in and the gate. Is there any reason why your uh, partner – you weren't married? – would have boarded the plane and then left it?'

'I don't think so. He wanted to come home. He had a symposium to go to.'

' Were either of you in financial difficulty?'

'No, certainly not.'

'Did your partner take out any lifc insurancc, recently?'

'He bought policies when we first moved in together.'

'Your partner was returning from Las Vegas. Did he gamble?'

'That is what you go there for,' said Steve.

'Yes,' said Jemma. 'But he rarely loses and never makes a big wager. It's more about the odds with him.'

'Did your partner have a drink problem or use any illegal substances?'

'No.'

'Did your partner hold any strong religious or political opinions?'

'What has that got to do with anyone?' demanded Steve.

'None.'

'Had he been abroad recently?'

'He has family in England. We spent the holidays there.'

'How did you meet?'

'At Brown.'

'What was his immigration status?'

'He is a citizen. And proud of it.'

He looked at Steve and back again. 'How was your relationship?'

'That's enough,' said Steve.

'The relationship is good. Or it will be when I get him back.'

'You refer to your partner in the present tense.'

'He is alive.'

'That is enough,' said Steve, again.

'If he contacts you we need to know immediately. Here's my card,' the investigator said and then he left with his silent partner.

'They're trying to screw with your mind,' said Steve.

'I know,' said Jemma. 'And I'm beginning to think that crazy guy Bob might have been right after all. If Mike was dead they would've out and told us,' she added. 'What are they doing to him?'

Mike began his daily routine of yoga stretches and calisthenics: greeting the sun, calf-raises, sit-ups and push-ups, all accomplished in the space next to his bed. If he was being watched it was not obvious. He had searched the room throughout. Whenever he looked out of the door he could see a guard moving around in the corridor or sitting on chair a little ways up.

The guard brought food but did not speak. Mike had no idea what to say, so said nothing. The guard brought an omelet with small pieces of processed ham and cheese in it, and a glass of orange juice, the reconstituted type. The bread roll was warm as if it had just been baked and it smelt good. Physically, he was improving but he was bored and anxious. Above all, his memory was starting to waken but in a way that made no more sense than his captivity. For the most part, his mind was an empty, monochrome lunar landscape but he was beginning to see objects among the rocks. There was a woman. Dark skinned, beautiful. She was both found and lost like paragraphs in a redacted document. His lack of memory made keeping track of time almost impossible. The man in the white coat had yet to supply a name. There was no daylight. They were probably below ground. Inside a vessel of some sort? There was no discernible movement, so not likely. Was his memory tantalizing him because he was being drugged? If he was part of an experiment, it was a strange one. And he was pretty sure he hadn't volunteered for it. Here was Hypnos, the cave in the underworld; here was the Lethe, whose waters wash away memory. Time to go.

Mike guessed the guard would come back in again in about 30 minutes to collect the plate. He thought about trying to overpower the guard or wrest the Taser from him and disable him or use him as a hostage. The guard almost certainly had skills and training that Mike lacked and he was bound to be stronger. Besides, Mike did not know how to work a Taser. He would probably take a punch to the throat while he was figuring it out.

When the guard took the plate, Mike waited for a count of 10 and then made his way out into the corridor, turning left as he exited the cell. He paused at the end of the corridor and listened for the creak of sole on vinyl. It looked like he had guessed right and the guard had gone to a kitchen station or a canteen somewhere out of hearing.

There were two doors at the end of the next branch of corridor. One had a handle and an electronic lock operated by a swipe card. The other led into nothing more interesting than an empty storeroom. Its door was closed but the latch had not taken and he was able to push it open. As he did so, he heard the distinctive squeak of the guard's boots and he slipped into the storeroom, leaving its door open a crack. The guard was carrying two large plastic sacks, probably garbage. He put one down to use the swipe card, pulled the door open and held it like that with his boot before negotiating his way through the doorway.

The door also had a closer and was shutting slowly enough for Mike to grab the handle and slip through. Ahead, metal steps led to a heavy door. Mike tried it. The door was unlocked so he slipped through that and continued in the same direction until he reached another set of metal steps and another door. This, too, was unlocked but rather than lead into a corridor, it opened in to a huge hangar-like space, a cavern quarried from salmon pink rock. Along the edge, where Mike skulked, there were high storage bays, mainly filled with wooden crates on pallets. He moved forward warily and found that ahead were rows of shipping containers in a double tier.

Mike peered round the edge of a container and caught a glimpse of a large silver object with a smooth skin and rounded edges. He edged forward but caught a movement out of the side of his eye. He pulled back into the shadow. As he listened, he could hear the sound of motors, and voices, from the other side of the space. He edged forward again until he had a better view of the metal object. It was an old twelve-wheeler Airstream trailer, a long, cigar-shaped structure clad in shiny aluminum. There was a set of antennae on the roof. One hung on a cable over its side, like a broken wing.

The noise from across the hangar was the loading of an odd assortment of vehicles on to big semis. They included a battered old red Sierra he had seen before. Somewhere.

A group of three men in the same gray fatigues as the guards, were guiding a truck as it reversed towards the spot where Mike crouched. The Airstream seemed the only place to hide. He yanked on the door handle and clambered in. It had been completely torn apart inside but there were still places to hide and he tucked himself into the space where a table had stood. He waited for about twenty minutes as various commands were barked and lines were attached to the trailer.

Mike felt the Airstream wallow as the driver's door opened. He shrank himself down into the gap as someone climbed. The cursory check took seconds but they dragged frame by frame.

After a shout of 'ready' the trailer gave a lurch. Mike had stowed away on a piggy-backed vehicle.

The Airstream lurched, pitched and rolled as the truck ground its way along a dirt road, chucking up a cloud of dust. They were in the desert somewhere, driving down from mountains toward a flat plain populated with desert sage, rabbit brush and grasses. That much Mike could see by snatching a look through the windows of the trailer. His view was mainly of empty sky.

There was a heap of clothes, with pockets turned out and linings ripped. Mike pulled a sweatshirt and a pair of pants over his pajamas and looked round for some shoes.

He was squeezing the boots on to his feet when he had to bob down. A military helicopter was keeping pace with them. A soldier was signaling to the driver to stop. As the truck braked, the helicopter swooped upwards and ahead to a spot where it could land. The truck halted. Mike was not going to wait for them to take him back to his white room. He slid the Airstream's side door open as narrow as he could, closed it carefully, slipped over the side of the low-loader, then ducked and ran to a stand of desert sage and crawled into a dip in the ground.

Mike could hear shouts and the sibilant thrum of the idling helicopter. He guessed they were searching the R.V.

He waited, expecting to look up into the barrel of a gun but it did not happen.

As hc heard the helicopter taking off he pushed himself beneath the blooming sage. It rewarded him with shelter and bathed him in its sweet, pungent aroma.

Chapter Eight

Majestic takes charge

Washington, D.C. 1958

From what Reeder had been able to piece together from conversations not just with high-flyers but also with the 'invisible people' around the President like Floyd Boring, Ike still relished the idea of Oppenheimer being stripped of his security clearance back in fifty-four. If anyone was going to carry the can for the Castle Bravo fiasco it was that subversive son of a gun. No matter the aliens struck a deal and so far it was holding, if not very productive. Oppenheimer could not be trusted. He and Albert Einstein had apparently written to Truman in 1947 urging the President not to antagonize the aliens. They knew more about them than Truman, who may have been many things but was still President. Besides, the F.B.I. had been keeping tabs on Oppenheimer since the Thirties, long before he was involved with the Manhattan Project. If not a card-carrying communist, like his brother, he was a fellow traveler. A disgrace.

No sooner had Truman declared that the U.S.A. would build an H-Bomb to stay ahead of the Soviets, than who should pop up but J. Robert Oppenheimer? – and he had thoroughly undermined all efforts to develop one ever since. The doubts he sowed had prevented the Bikini bomb test ahead of the meeting with the E.B.Es. Who knows what kind of a deal we might have got if we had been able to make a show of strength? When that bomb blew on 1 March 1954, the world shook. A yield of fifteen megatons of T.N.T., a thousand times more destructive power than the bombs dropped on Hiroshima and Nagasaki. Oppenheimer and his monkeys at Los Alamos had predicted that it would be one-third that size. When the boys at Bikini got their slide rules out they panicked. Of course they did. Before Trinity, they were all scared we would set fire to the atmosphere and wipe ourselves out in a huge fireball.

Reeder knew Ike favoured Cray. He had been the chairman of the Atomic Energy Commission board who recommended that Oppenheimer be cast into the wilderness. The last Reeder heard, Oppenheimer was playing at being a farm hand in Colorado. Cray, by contrast, was now Ike's appointee as National Security Advisor, a key man and no-one, not even the Senate, could stand in his way because his was a staff position. He was also something on some committee or other codenamed Majestic.

What Reeder could not know at that point was that an arrangement had been made with E.B.E.s and it seemed to be working in the sense that human race had not been conquered or enslaved, even though Majestic had yet to see the promised transfer of technology. Ike believed they could still hold up their end of the deal as long as Earth provided a suitable haven. It was ironic that when it finally took place the Bikini test had contributed to Majestic fulfilling a major part of the treaty bargain. The blast had vaporized the buildings equipment that were supposed to send back data; the radioactive fallout had dropped on an area a hundred miles long including inhabited islands and it had caused an international incident with Japan by poisoning the crew of a fishing vessel. The upshot was that the U.S. was under pressure to end atmospheric tests and carry them out underground. The E.B.Es' demands included a base. Cray advised that underground testing would enable the U.S. to try out more devices but also to excavate under New Mexico or Nevada, away from large human populations and prying eyes. It would be a hell of a project and ways would have to be found to maintain secrecy over the cost and materials involved in any construction work, a landing strip, some underground hangars, repair facilities, a bunker and accommodation hidden away inside a mountain. An added difficulty was that the alien craft appeared on radar. The solution had been to instruct military air controllers to report all radar incidents. They became so commonplace that filing a report and forgetting about it was routine. But the aliens were harder to instruct. They flew where they damn well liked. Building a base would make it easier to limit their movements. The Majestic group would see to that. Ike had not given them carte blanche but he now kept the committee at arm's length. Since becoming D.C.I. a couple of years back, Allen Dulles had been persuasive of the need for Ike to be able, plausibly, to deny knowledge of either Majestic or the treaty, if not on constitutional or even financial grounds, simply because it gave the U.S. the edge. With his lawyer's hat on, Dulles had pointed out the precedent set by Harry Truman with the N.S.C. paper on covert operations 'so planned and executed that any U.S. Government responsibility for them is not evident to unauthorized persons and that if uncovered the U.S. Government can plausibly disclaim any responsibility for them'.

The Majestic group's presumption had riled Ike at first but right now the situation suited him; his gut was playing up again and he had found himself short of breath on more than one occasion recently. He had once been fit – athletic even – so feeling the sand run out was a harsh blow. There's one enemy you can never beat.

The E.B.E.s' second demand, seemed harmless enough: to learn more about humans. According to the verbal briefings Ike received each month our 'space brothers' had take to selecting individuals, seemingly at random, to take them on joy rides in their spacecraft. At least that was part of the current folklore promulgated among flying saucer folk. The C.I.A. were happy to encourage tales of that sort, as long as they didn't get out of hand. Most of the so-called 'contactees' were delusional fabulists or simply people who had been driven to embroider a lie into a tale. U.F.O. activity observed by cooler, better-trained heads – military heads – was subject to continuing scrutiny by the Air Force's Project Blue Book team, whose brief was to find credible explanations for the events, come what may. So far, so good, except…

Majestic convened at a new location each time. Each member traveled on his own using at least two forms of transport, and arrived and left by a back entrance. They had been briefed to check for unfamiliar automobiles near their homes and offices, to walk slowly and to stop from time to time to see if they were being followed, without looking round. As the committee arrived, Beetle Smith and Gordon Cray were already waiting, and they looked worried. Hynek, the astronomer, had been co-opted, along with Lieutenant Colonel Corso and Allen Dulles.

Cray was anxious to get going. 'Gentlemen, we have had to put the alien situation under review. General Smith, as negotiator, will fill you in on recent developments.'

'I regret to say that say that the benefits we had hoped for from our treaty with the aliens have not so far been forthcoming,' Smith began. 'Setting up negotiations has proven difficult and they are often inconclusive. Despite early, rapid progress, agreeing any kind of timetable or goal seems to be beyond them and furthermore they have begun to make new demands, which I do not believe we should acquiesce in until we have seen concrete results from our treaty. Our major problem is that we have failed to apply a basic lesson: know thine enemy.'

'We should never have signed the treaty,' chimed in Corso.

'That is as maybe,' said Smith.

'What are these changes and what difference will they make?' asked Lloyd Birkener.

Twining answered. 'Among all the other reports of alien encounters, we are getting more that are difficult to write off as natural phenomena or the ravings of lunatics. Most contactees are attention-seekers but we've actually found a number who are doing quite the opposite. They're extremely reluctant to describe their meeting with aliens – which, I might add, are highly credible – for reasons I personally find very sinister.'

Dulles spoke. 'Our guys have had some of them in and put them on a truth serum, and used a lie detector on them. They appear to be telling the truth.'

'Sodium thiopental, seems very effective at suppressing the higher cortical functions of the brain, which, oddly, impairs lying,' said Bronk.

'Get to the point,' said Cray.

Dulles spoke again. 'Gordon, these people have been abducted by the creatures and subjected to experimentation. It's all in here.' He handed Cray a file.

Hynek looked uncomfortable. 'I, myself, have also spoken to a number of contactees. They have tended to come to me and so in that sense they are a self-selecting group but they almost all reported encounters that were benign in nature. In their accounts the aliens mainly appeared curious, almost naïve, and had not harmed the contactees in any way, although contactees were often left many miles from home, dazed and disheveled. There has been an odd turn of events. First, these people are more likely to report that the aliens are communicating with them telepathically. They are reading their minds and, in a sense, writing on them too.'

'They communicate with us through that device of theirs,' said Smith. 'Could they be reading our minds at the same time?'

'If we were to accept the premise that telepathic communication is possible, and other than these reports we have no evidence that it is, then yes, they could be,' said Vannever Bush.

'Well, that would explain why we have done so badly,' said Birkener.

'Secondly,' said Hynek, 'the nature of these "conversations" has changed. Where previously contactees said they asked questions about their age and the size of their families and so on, the aliens are now conversing on what might be described as a deeper level. Namely, they ask questions about crime, war and even notions of property and wealth. The conversations generally lead to an expression of the wish to see mankind abandon atomic weaponry.'

The military men around the table flinched as one. 'How long before they make a direct demand to us, to disarm?' wondered General Hoyt Vandenberg.

'And how long before they attack, if we are defenseless,' said Corso.

‘They have not shown signs of aggression so far. They may have genuine motivations towards peace,’ said Bush.

‘They may have a genuine motivation towards turning our population sissy,’ said Smith. ‘These attempts to brainwash our people into pacifism are very disturbing. It needs to be countered.’

‘Thirdly,’ Hyenk continued, ‘they seem to be taking a rather unsavory interest in our sex lives: how we procreate and so on.’

‘Have the aliens gone any further?’ asked a shocked Birkener.

‘It is my belief,’ said Bronk, ‘that we are no longer with the benign aliens that President Eisenhower met at Edwards. I was present at the most recent set of negotiations and note physical differences between the creatures on that occasion and the extraterrestrials we first encountered. They were somewhat larger. If the original creatures were four foot tall, these are at least half a foot taller. Their physiognomy is changing. Their noses are more pronounced and they appear to have a septum which the others lacked. We have also realized that they have nictitating membrane over their eyes, a second eyelid, like a cat’s, presumably to deal with some atmospheric condition on their planet. We did not observe them blinking before. We could be dealing with a different type of alien or this could simply be that we are dealing with more mature specimens. You may be familiar with the orangutan, pongo pygmaeus, a species of primate found in Borneo and Sumatra. On maturity the male changes his appearance quite dramatically and develops cheek pouches that substantially alter his appearance…'

'Fascinating as this is,' Cray interrupted, 'Majestic's immediate concern is to ensure that these aliens come good on their promise to provide us with their technology. What bearing does this have?'

'Please stay with me,' said Bronk. 'If these are simply a more mature version of the creatures we have been dealing with, their behavior may be changing as a result of hormonal differences. In many Earth species males in particular become more aggressive when they reach physical adulthood. They obviously get more interested in sex and… '

Dulles broke in. 'Claims have been made that aliens are abducting humans.'

It took a moment for the group to register what he had said. Then there was a clamor. When it died down Dulles explained: 'We used truth serum of five subjects who made an allegation of this type and with some variation they all give accounts that follow a pattern. These abductions begin with a sighting of an alien craft either in the air or, in one case, on the ground. We believe this may be a reconnaissance. Significantly, gentlemen, these contactees are rendered powerless by some means we have yet to discover, which may be a gas, a type of ray or it could be through mind control. It is imperative that we understand the means of control in order to assess our vulnerability. I would press for this weapon or ability to be disclosed to us as a priority, General Smith, when and if meaningful negotiations take place.' He paused. 'If we had it, it could be extremely useful as a means of subduing hostile individuals or even whole populations. These putative abductees report being taken from their homes or, often fields, to what we believe must be inside their crafts. We have so far been unable to glean any useful information about the capabilities of these craft, how they are equipped or propelled. I gather you have some idea about that though, Smith?'

Birkener fidgeted. 'What do they do to them in there?'

Dulles resumed. 'They appear to be carrying out medical examinations, possibly under hypnosis. The examinations are thorough, intimate and in at least one case are alleged to have involved surgery, although no scars were found. They seem oddly interested in the sex organs.'

'Of course this could all be neurotic fantasy,' said Hyenk. 'But it is very worrying, nevertheless.'

'Our medics believe the aliens are interested in the hormonal system of humans,' said Dulles.

'For God's sake tell me they aren't considering miscegenation,' said Bush. 'Some sort of hybridization?'

'Cross-breeding? Mating with humans?' mused Hyenk. 'Who knows? They are a long way from home.'

'Shore leave!' laughed Admiral Hillenkoetter.

'No. If we are talking about them seeding themselves in humans as a way to survive here or to colonize us I seriously doubt it would work,' Hyenk said slowly. 'We are far too far apart evolutionarily. Who knows how life developed where they come from? We know that even species that are close seldom cross-breed effectively. Think of the mule. It is a dead-end in terms of perpetuating the species.'

'But they still exist – because we make it happen,' said Birkener. 'We take the jenny to the stallion.'

'That is true. But the chances of it working between species from different planets is so remote it is, excuse the pun, astronomical,' said Hyenk. 'Personally I would find the idea that they might do it to for pleasure, far more disturbing.'

'May I conjecture,' said Bronk. 'If they are interested in hormones it may be because they lack something, perhaps as a result of a prolonged change in diet or they may simply be looking for a way to extend their longevity or even need it as an aphrodisiac. It could be their equivalent of monkey gland treatment. You remember Vronoff? He started by transplanting thyroid glands from chimpanzees into humans and then did a pretty good trade in grafting tissue from one set of testicles to another. To begin with, he used executed criminals as a source but when they ran out he took the tissue from chimps and baboons. Made a fortune from millionaires who would have done better having tissue inserted into their brains instead of their scrotums.'

'Please! This is revolting,' said Birkener.

Hillenkoetter had clearly had a thought. 'If they are in the market for hormones, we have a bargaining chip. The same goes for them getting a piece of human tail. If we can buy a mind control weapon by selling a few asses, that's a pretty good trade. We can source them down south.'

'You're talking about pandering our people to another species,' roared Birkener.

'Not "our" people, obviously,' said Hillenkoetter.

'Gentlemen, we do not even know if they have distinct sexes. They might be hermaphrodites for all we know, or parthenogenic, self-reproducing. We simply do not know.'

'What about the ones you examined at Roswell?'

'We learned very little. We had very little to work on. The samples were decomposing as we examined them. As far as we could see, there was an absence of recognizable genitalia but we had no idea what we were looking at or looking for. We have not witnessed them eat or defecate, let alone reproduce. We don't even have scat to examine. All we know is that they do need water, though what they do with it is not clear; they like the warmth but they don't like plain sunshine. What would I give to get another of these creatures on the table?' said Bronk.

'Before we start cutting them up, we should look into what would make them hand over the secret of mind control,' said Cray. 'Beetle. Let me know the minute they request another meeting. We need to know if we are dealing with a different set of aliens, in which case we may be able to reach a more productive arrangement with them. Until we are sure of our ground we will not need to trouble the President. We can handle this ourselves.'

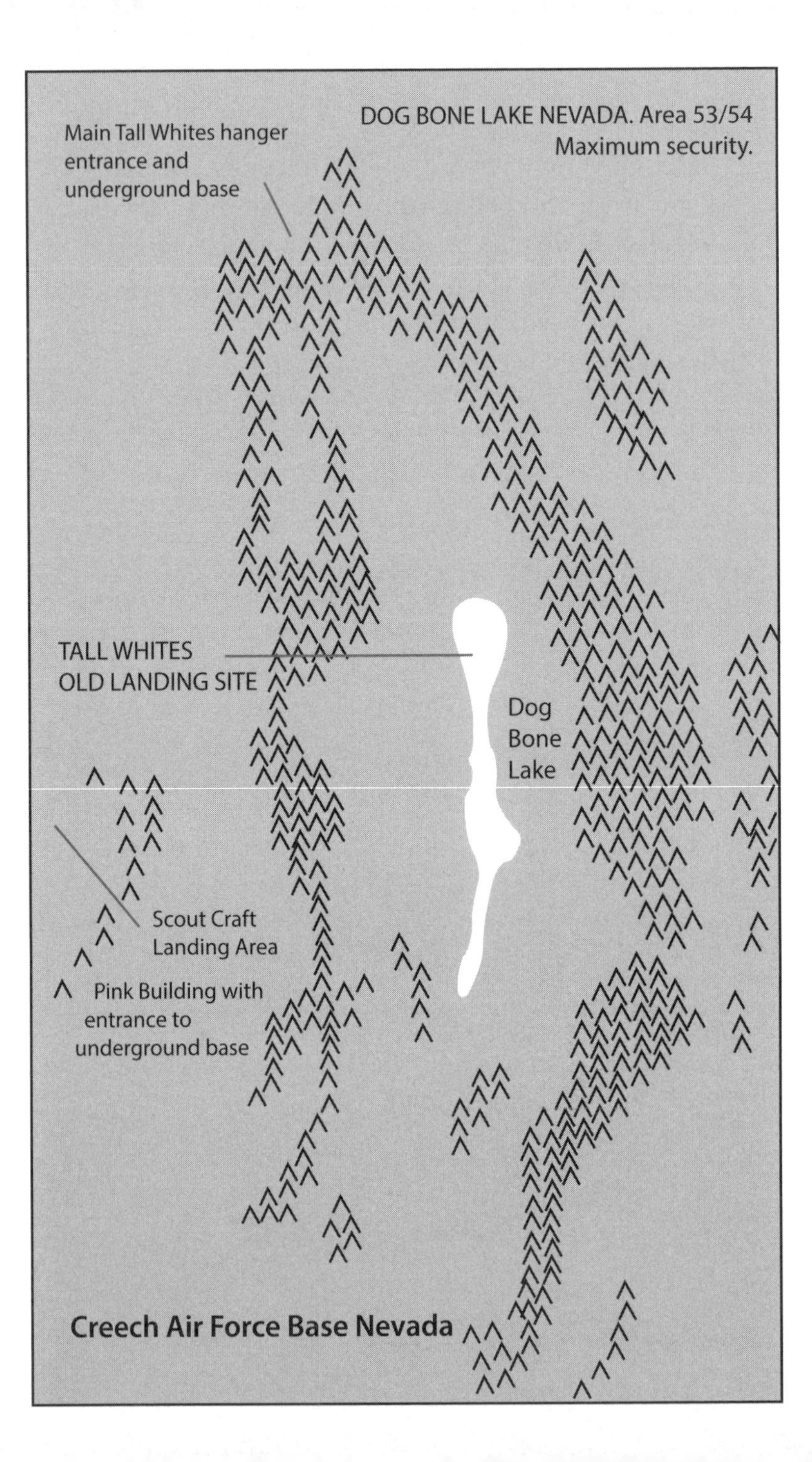
DOG BONE LAKE NEVADA. Area 53/54
Maximum security.
Main Tall Whites hanger
entrance and
underground base
TALL WHITES
OLD LANDING SITE
Dog
Bone
Lake
Scout Craft
Landing Area
Pink Building with
entrance to
underground base
Creech Air Force Base Nevada

Chapter Nine

Drone Chase

Dog Bone Lake, NV. Present

It was dark, near dawn, when Mike shivered himself awake, still in the embrace of the sagebrush. Its scent permeated his borrowed clothes and his hair. He knelt and surveyed the area as best he could in the half-light. He was not far from the road. Against the gently glowing sky he could make out a power line stretched over the desert. He would find humanity in some form at either end. As it ran at diagonals to the road, he chose to follow it away from the direction in which he had come. He stood to test his legs and found they were steady.

The boots pinched but were better than the slippers he had been wearing. Damn, he thought as he realized he had left them in the trailer. Would they be spotted when it reached its destination? Would whoever found them figure that he had been aboard and where he must have jumped out?

He began walking as fast as could without tripping, mainly trying to watch the ground ahead but looking up from time to time to check his bearings. As he moved, he picked up more of the scent and he had a distinct sense of déjà vu. Was it an illusion or had he walked somewhere very like this before? Surely all the desert would look much the same in this light. When would he have been there and why? Wondering made him lose concentration and stumble. He felt weaker and suddenly thirsty. He found a rock to rest on and catch his breath, then began to piece together what he had been doing when he was last in a place like this.

He remembered they had been pointed out into the desert, the worse for having drunk a lot of beer, and had found a spot to watch the sky at some time around midnight. They had cooled off and sobered up. The conversation had taken a philosophical turn and… His memory jinked and Mike suddenly remembered Jemma. His Jemma. Her voice on the phone. His hand on her cheek just before he turned to take a taxi. He felt alone for the first time. It was not a sensation he had experienced in his cell but out here under the sky and so far from her, he felt more than alone: deeply lonely. Why was he here and she… at their home? Their home? Where? It would come. He knew it would come.

A light breeze made the grass riffle. And he remembered something else: the strange-looking kid and the red haired woman at the Space Station. 'Oh looky here,' she had said. 'You couldn't have had a close encounter by any chance?'

The overhead line ran as far as the eye could see across the range. It could stretch for dozens of miles but it was Mike's best hope of finding help, so he followed it without deviating. He knew that wandering away from it would be fatal. The clothes he wore were tight and the boots were at least a size too small. While they afforded some protection he could feel the rough ground beneath his feet and he trudged forward. He was tiring and his throat was bone dry. When he looked around, the air shimmered but it was not a mirage, it was his vision that was wrong. He blinked consciously but could feel the sting of sweat on his eyes. He rested but dared not do so for too long: 'To sleep, to die and in that sleep what dreams may come'. Snatches of memory. A line of a tune. The sound of rain, of cheering from the bleachers, of the sea crashing on shores of Cape Cod and the beach in England with its light house flashing patiently and the red and white lights of aircraft passing overhead, and Jemma – Jemma laughing, joyously, at a summer barbecue, laughing uproariously at some joke he had missed, his incomprehension making her giggle and guffaw all the more. And kissing. And lying together on plush grass and looking at the stars. Was that perspiration or tears burning his eyes? He grew even more tired, jarring with pain now at every step.

That child. That child had held up a strange, malformed hand to protect itself. He remembered now. That child held up a long thin hand, like a frond of seaweed tugged by the current. It had formed its mouth into a silent scream. Why was it so scared? And that hand? What was wrong with that hand? Disease? Some terrible accident? And it's alabaster face and almond-shaped eyes. Such an odd, sad, frightened creature, almost a lost faun. His instinct had been to protect it, to help it, but it clearly feared him. What was it doing out there so far from anywhere and where had it come from?

Mike lowered himself on to a rock and touched the ground. He had felt the dirt under his hand that day too as he lay there suffering waves of nausea and shivering himself into movement. At first, he could not move at all. His field of view was a weave of green and gray and purple; the only sound he could hear: the rustle of the grass in a light breeze.

As he sat there, and tried to picture that day, he became aware of the rapid switching and clicking. He had wandered into a rattlesnake's home territory. He knew snakes are deaf. It must have sensed his presence from his footfall. He moved his head slowly to listen and judge where the rattler was lurking, and, then, very slowly, moved away step by step. The temperature was rising and they would be more active now. He recalled a documentary Doug had made on snakes in California. Doug! Were they looking for him? Surely they were. They did. They always did.

Mike pressed on, walking painfully, for hours and fearing to stop in case he could not restart. As evening approached, he could feel the warmth beneath him radiating into the air and even the breeze began to pinch. It made him shiver. He had gone as far as he could. He lowered himself on to the dirt and sank his head between his knees. He must rise. Must move. As the ground became more rugged he found himself grudgingly traipsing up a slope. It gave him a perch. As he searched to find some strength, he perceived a glow from above. Had the moon appeared? There were no clouds just a huge sky whitewashed with billions of cold-looking, white-hot dots smeared on an incomprehensibly vast backdrop of black. But there was light, a warm white glow from above. As Mike looked up, he could see the stars vanish as if a veil was being pulled over the sky. It appeared to meld into a single canopy.

He sensed that there was movement: a smooth transit of something massive that stretched in all directions. If it were low overhead, Mike calculated, it would be at least the size of a baseball field. Mike's mind spun. For a second, he could see himself at Fenway Park, roaring on the Red Sox. He refocused and began to search for the outline of this phenomenon. As it gradually and, seemingly slowly, passed over, Mike could see that it was pear-shaped and what looked, at first, like a smooth surface was covered in striations. It made no sound but Mike could feel the air warming gently. The glow was from a hot surface. His mind whirled and bucked. Was he seeing what he thought he was seeing? The impossible? The fantastically, crazily, mind-bendingly improbable? A spacecraft? A giant ship holding itself in the sky and glowing from its entry into the atmosphere, Earth's atmosphere?

The strength that had drained from him returned. He moved swiftly and determinedly in the direction of travel of the craft, driven by unalloyed curiosity to run and scramble up the slope. At its peak, he saw the craft begin to duck between two ranges of hills divided by a dry lake. The ship appeared to be about to drive itself into the rock of the lakebed.

Mike pictured the black and white footage he had seen on TV as a boy: The Hindenburg catching fire and falling from the sky before it crashed and folded in a surge of flames. And Herbert Morrison's radio report of the final moments of the airship and its passengers: 'It's crashing. Terrible! Oh, my! Get out of the way. Please! It's burning and bursting into flames…' He was struck with a horrifying thought: might that be what he was about to witness? Might he be swept up in the conflagration? The craft continued tipping on its nose like a sinking ship and began to move towards the lakebed. Unable to take in what he was seeing, Mike watched as the craft gradually passed through the lake floor as it were a fog. For a moment, he wondered if it might be folding into itself like the fake knife he had as a kid, whose blade would disappear into its hilt. But it was passing through the surface and, after about a minute, disappeared altogether.

As he ran the image back and forth through his brain, trying to make sense of it, his eyes began to take in details of the lake area and he could see a straight line running up one side of the lakebed. This had to be manmade. A path. A power line? He could not tell from here. He calculated that it would take him at least three hours to reach it in his current condition but it was only the second sign of human activity he had seen since his escape. There might be some form of habitation close by, and water.

Mike began a slow, excruciating descent. A rock slipped from beneath his step and skittered downwards, sending him off-balance. The pain was instant as the sharp rock slashed his hand. It bled furiously. He held it above his head. The outer pocket on the shredded jacket was hanging off; he ripped it away and used it to staunch the cut. Getting somewhere safe, finding water, was vital. He could not do this for much longer. He righted himself and scrambled slowly down the slope, checking the location of the line, stopped and studied again. This time, he saw a flash at the side of his eye and looked skywards to see four fast-moving balls of lights. One came to a halt in the sky and then one after another they began a descent at an angle that roughly matched that of the strata in rocks behind – a little over fifty degrees he estimated – towards the lakebed. Mike watched as they too penetrated its floor – with no damage to themselves and no disturbance that he could see to the surface. It was extraordinary. The surface was neither solid nor liquid. A plasma? Generated around the vehicle? A skin of plasma, unstable perhaps or with an incredibly low electron density? He began to dig around in his mind. You would use a Poisson equation to calculate its field strength. The math governing plasmas was straight forward but visualizing their behavior was way, way too complex. 'Impossible,' he realized. 'Good grief. I don't really even know how enough to calculate their speed. That has to be the simplest calculation, let alone... Vlasov-Maxwell! Hold that thought. Hold that thought!'

The fourth craft appeared to hang back before its descent. It followed the same line and angle but, as it closed on the lake, it seemed to pull up and instead of entering the lakebed; bounced and skipped across its surface like a pebble skimming a pond, sending up a cloud of dust instead of spray and finally cart-wheeling and coming to halt in the distance. Rather than explode, it grew dimmer and, oddly, Mike felt his headache disappear as if the craft crashing had thrown a switch extinguishing both it and his line of thought. The craft spun to halt. Far in the distance, it appeared to be intact but inert.

Mike looked back at the edge of the lake to get his bearings again and noticed that there was movement along his datum line. Tiny-looking vehicles were pouring out of a point hidden from his view, at the far end of the line, across the lakebed and towards the craft. Mike tried to triangulate the point from features in the hills on both sides. That was where he needed to go. He was numb and stiff but he focused on that one point and began mechanically to make his way towards it step after step. The rocks became looser and more treacherous. They became scree. It slipped and slid beneath his wary tread. He lurched, flailing his ragged arms like a manic drunk, trying to stay upright. Eventually, the land flattened out and he felt the even surface of a dirt road beneath his sole. It was rolled dead flat but also stained with a seemingly random pattern of dark lines: a Jackson Pollack creation designed to mimick shadows and make it appear broken and rough, even from just a short distance. He followed it towards his goal, keeping to the hillward side of the road and looking out for hiding places. The road curved slightly. He began to perceive a tall entrance like the mouth of a huge pipe, in the side of the hill. This must have been where the vehicles came from. He could see a line of lights on the ceiling.

As he moved closer, he kept a wary eye open for movement. He needed help but if he were ever to see Jemma again he knew that he must avoid recapture. He was not about to end his days in that white room.

A military vehicle screeched from the tunnel and out in the direction of the crashed craft. Mike edged towards the tunnel until he could get a look inside. He entered, staying close to one wall, bathed in a hellish red light, The tunnel, alone, could easily house a trio of jumbo jets, nose to tail. As he went deeper, it broadened into a vast cavern in which were three craft, presumably the smaller ones that he had seen landing through the lakebed before, resting like eggs balanced on their sides, nose, or tail down. Had they come through the tunnel? he wondered. He edged closer. They were silent and cold and immobile. He leant forward to touch the skin of one. It was silky, without a blemish. There were no rivets or seams, nor windows or rocket exhausts. As he ran a hand over the craft's surface, an ear-piercing whistle filled the air. It deepened into the howl of a klaxon, then a baritone rumble.

Mike pressed himself into the wall of the cavern. It

gave way behind him, sending him sprawling into a new space. His feet appeared to be inside the glass-smooth rock. He drew them up. Turning and crawling forward, he probed the wall with his good hand. It folded around his fingers. There was no sensation of solidity; it was as if it were a hologram or a projection – but he knew it was real. 'I refute it thus'. Yet, with his heart racing, he held his breath and shuffled forward, and he passed through the mist-like wall, a hank of cloth dragging across the rock floor as he crawled.

When he reached the new space he felt a tug at his leg. The cloth was embedded in the wall. He pulled at it hard and the cuff of his pants parted in a ragged ring. The fabric remained embedded. The wall was absolutely solid. It had changed state. Had he been a fraction slower he would have been a fossil. A cold sweat ran down his back.

He could see points of light further down. They seemed to stretch forever into the distance, as small as stars. They ran along the side of a huge pipe that held about two feet above the ground and had heavy-duty insulated cables running along its side, gathered in swags at points about ten yards apart. He put his hand up to towards the pipe's surface. It was icy cold. If he touched it, his skin would stick to the surface and he would only free himself by tearing a chunk from his hand. The air was close but cool. He must keep moving. But which way? The pipe seemed to stretch endlessly in both directions. He chose the one he was facing in and began to walk.

After what he thought must have been about two miles he saw a different, warmer light in the distance. As he got closer he crouched and listened. He could hear voices. Two men in hard hats appeared from the gap in the tunnel wall that let the light in and they started moving away from where Mike was guided by flashlights. He stumbled towards the light. It was a door with a window of meshed glass. Inside was what looked like a small kitchen with an eating area comprising a table and four chairs. There was refrigerator, a sink and a coffee maker. Mike opened a cupboard and found a mug. It almost slipped from his fingers as he tried to grip it under the faucet. He drank. The water felt like an icy rod pushed down his throat and yet he felt as if a huge weight had been lifted off his chest. The refrigerator was stacked with cellophane-wrapped sandwiches. He took four and stuffed them into what was left of the pockets of his jacket. There was an empty plastic bottle in the bin under the sink and he took that and rinsed it out and filled it. Then, he grabbed another sandwich and ate it. It filled him immediately, to the point of making him feel sick, but he keep eating.

The room was warmer and he was tempted to sit down and rest his head – but sleep would be dangerous. There was no telling when those men would come back or who they would bring with them. He came out of the office and turned back the way he came so that he would not run into them. He would have to turn back. After about five miles, with the tunnel exactly the same all along its length, he reached a side passage. It went just a short distance to another huge cavern filled with what looked like large vats. Men were working at height on them. He edged along the wall towards another doorway. It too led to another area, this time filled with deep tanks of liquid. He kept exploring, finding a dark corner to curl up in when he was too exhausted to move further. He had no idea how long each had been there. His first two sandwiches had gone quickly but when he realized how far this underground complex stretched, he knew he would have to take them out. He needed more water. His mouth was dry and his head thumped. Maybe there would be another office somewhere, where he could drink. At last, he found another door and opened it, peering round it cautiously. He could see stars and felt a light breeze on his face. It was a door to the outside world. An unlocked door to the desert.

He limped as hard as he could, out towards the road. It all seemed clear. But then he heard a shout – not a call, an order – behind him. Then, another shout. One word. 'Halt!' He knew a shot would follow. There was a loud crack. Mike hobbled, ducked, into the dark until he found a rock. He crouched behind it. His chest burnt and his throat felt as if a tree had been thrust down it. There was barely room for the air. His skull felt like it had shrunk. A searchlight played over the rocks as a Hummer drove slowly along the road. Its beam rested on the rock that hid Mike. He froze as it lingered there but it moved off and the search continued.

The sky was streaked with red. As Mike scanned it he saw something crossing it. At first, he mistook the drone for a bat until he saw that it was trailing an object that swung when it changed direction or speed. The drone followed the edge of the lakebed. Then it stopped in mid-air. Its cargo hung beneath as it moved directly and precisely to where Mike hid. It moved in an arc above his head, then began to lower the object. Back in the control center, Lemmy steeled himself to fire up the Coyame weapon. But along with Mike's thermal signature among the rocks he could see three others close by. Colder. Taller. 'Back off,' he said under his breath. 'Back the hell off.' But instead of moving away, they closed in on Mike.

Mike heard their approach. He was way too tired to crawl, let alone run. He looked up and saw three preternaturally gangly figures. These were the tall men he had seen before. It was as if they had materialized from a dream, a nightmare. The angels of death. Horror mounted in him as he braced for paralysis and pain. But it did not come. They surrounded him and then folded their arms around one another to form a strange, living canopy over him.

Lemmy gasped as he saw the four heat signatures merge on his screen.

'Stand down!' barked Kirby. 'They're shielding him.'

Brandy had dug out some photocopies she'd kept from Columbia; notes Douglas Reeder had bequeathed the library. They were in an ancient Manila folder of cuttings with the words 'Washington Flap' and 'Majority 12' just visible in pencil on the cover. Brandy assumed it was a reference to politics. The photocopies were of pages from a notebook that she had not really known how to treat at the time. There was also a print of a black and white photograph with a typed caption glued to it: 'President John F. Kennedy and General Curtis E. LeMay at the Swearing-In Ceremony of General LeMay as Chief of Staff of the United States Air Force.' Kennedy was shaking hands with LeMay on the steps of a building with columns and arched windows. Officials stood in two or three rows and looked on. A grease pencil arrow pointed to a bullet-headed man in a suit and shades, standing between two military figures. Few of the notebook's contents made sense to her. They spanned pretty much the whole of Douglas Reeder's long career right up to his mysterious disappearance in 1972, but from the mid-Fifties onward the pages were mostly cryptic lists, mainly of initials and acronyms, sometimes also of places. Some of the initials were easier to decipher than others such as J.F.K. and L.B.J. Kennedy's initials came up a lot toward the end of the book, long after his assassination, alongside some that were recognizable – E.W. was surely Earl Warren. R.N. or R.M.N. might be Richard Milhous Nixon. Then there were the obviously military ones. Lt Col P.C., Gen C.E.L. and so on. These others meant little, if anything, to her but clearly had significance to Douglas Reeder, given the under-scorings and the lines drawn around some of them. Why she hadn't seen it before she didn't know but the final entry was dated the very day Reeder vanished. Surely, it must only be coincidence that Doug Reeder's grandfather should have disappeared and now so too had his friend? It had to be, that is, if you believed in coincidence.

Mike was back in the white room. This time they were taking no chances. He was beyond resistance but in any case one arm was cuffed to the metal bed head and they had pumped him full of something to keep him tranquil. His head lolled like a broken puppet's. With an enormous effort, he looked around. Two forms shimmered into view: the bullet-headed man in the white coat, and a woman in a military uniform, an officer of some kind.

Kirby spoke first. 'You're lucky to be alive. If you want to remain that way you will have to behave. Do you understand what I am saying?'

Mike tried to concentrate on her but her face as it came in and out of focus. He heard a low moan and realized it was his own voice.

'What did you give him? He's barely functioning,' said the man in white. 'Don't you understand the risk you run if he dies. They have gone out of their way to protect him..'

'Our medics are trained for war, not this sort of thing,' said Kirby. 'Maybe he is having some kind of reaction?'

'You had better leave him with me. I'll let you know when he can communicate.'

Kirby nodded and left. The man in white waited until they were both sure she had gone.

'What happened out there?' he asked. 'From the beginning.'

For reasons Mike didn't entirely understand, he trusted this guy. His voice slowly returned. 'Before I got here, before I got out, I got lost in the desert. I found this kid, lost, right out there in the middle of nothing but when I went to help her, I got jumped by these guys who came from nowhere. They hit me with some kind of weapon that paralyzed me. My friends found me. I thought maybe I had some kind of dream or hallucination. Maybe some kind of seizure. But they were the same guys who brought me in this time. Really tall. If I believed in ghosts that's what I would say they were.'

'The child you helped is very special – particularly to the "people" who brought you in,' the man in white said. He sounded like he'd made a decision. 'Many of the things that have happened to you may have done so for a purpose. Where do you come from?'

'Boston.'

'No. Originally.'

'A place called Rendlesham Forest, in Suffolk, England.'

'What was it like?'

'Quiet, mostly. Rural. Fields. Woods. It's near Orford Ness on the North Sea. There is or was an American Air Base there at R.A.F. Woodbridge. The big Hercules planes used to come in low over our school. They passed directly overhead. Made a big noise. And massive great helicopters, too, with two props. Sikorskys. That was as exciting as it got. Not much happened.'

'Nothing that stands out? No event?'

'The only thing that stands out is Boxing Day, when I was in the fifth form. I was walking back over the fields from a mate's farm some time after tea, maybe about six o'clock or seven. We had been metal detecting. There's a lot of archeology there. Bronze Age through to Norman. It was pretty nippy, and dark, of course, but there was a completely clear sky and plenty of moonlight. I saw a plane, or maybe a helicopter, come down somewhere near the edge of the forest. I thought at first it was a shooting star. We used to see quite a few of those before the street lamps went in. The only light round there was the lighthouse at Orford, which you could see from miles away, and there were landing beacons at the other air base over at R.A.F. Bentwaters, which was also round there. There was a streak of light across the sky and then the aircraft came down near the edge of the forest, outside the fence at Woodbridge. That was a bit odd because clearly they were supposed to land on the base itself.

'The ground was hard but it was frosty and it was pretty slippery even where it had been plowed. I went as fast as I could across the field to see what had happened. There wasn't any blaze or anything like that and it may just have landed hard. But I wanted to see it. When I got there, I didn't really get to see it because I got hit by a real bright light. I have no idea where it came from but it was powerful and dazzling. I couldn't see a thing. Maybe it was a searchlight and I'd just looked straight into it. Anyway, all I could see was orange flashes and I tripped and twisted my ankle. When I could see again, there was nothing there and no-one around and it took me ages to get home. I couldn't have got back before about ten. My mum had conniptions when she saw the state of me and my dad had to step in. I was hopping about on that ankle for days. I saw a police car go up our lane but then that was it. Nothing in the paper or on the radio.'

'Did anything like that ever happen to you again?'

'Not for years.'

'But it did happen?'

'Yes. I came over here to do a master's after I went to Cambridge and I met Jemma at Brown in Rhode Island and then we moved to Boston when I got a lectureship. She has this thing about always going somewhere or doing something you've never done before. Where I came from it was flat, really flat so she fixed it for me and the guys to go skiing in Colorado. We were in the backcountry near a place called Silverton. It wasn't particularly cold. It was nice out there but I guess we should have known there was the danger of an avalanche. There were signs that there had been in the area. We could hear cracking noises from further up the slope. We were still above the tree line at about 11,000 feet when we reached a place where there were a lot of exposed rocks. The snow actually sounded kind of hollow and it was heavy-going.

'Something triggered an avalanche and in a matter of seconds I found myself being churned around in the dark. I tried to swim my way out of the cascade. It was real hard work and I got wrenched around and battered. It was brutal. I tried to do a kind of back crawl to get as far uphill as I could until the cascade started slowing down and I got my hands to my face to create an air pocket. I moved my hands to make it bigger. My mouth was full of snow so I spit and then I knew I was more or less upright, although I was lodged there. The snow was packed in around me and I couldn't move much, but I could breathe.

'It turned out that the other guys were OK. Gary skied out of the way of the avalanche. The two others were swept along on top of the debris, down into some trees, but they were not buried. They were doing fifty miles an hour at one point. It is amazing they didn't get smashed up. When they saw I was missing they started looking round for me but they were pretty disoriented.

'I have no idea how deep I was. I tried to keep calm. I hate small spaces. Potholing taught me that. It felt like I had been down there a hell of a long time and I was beginning to get light-headed. I guess I was breathing stale air although there might have been some coming in from above. It's kind of insane that I am alive. Gary said they were searching for nearly three hours, so I should have been dead from hypothermia or suffocation long, long before they found me. You don't last more than an hour in those conditions. Steve spotted one of my gloves on the surface and they took turns to dig and scrape away the snow, assuming I was dead. By then, other people had arrived and were helping. Someone put a probe down and found me and they moved about two tons of snow between them, digging in from just further down the slope to create a kind of tunnel.

'They were convinced they would find a corpse. But the weirdest thing: I was kind of going in and out of consciousness, which is not good, but I was alive and there was this really strong light. Like the light in Rendlesham. I think maybe it was hypoxia but it was a kind of near-death experience in all senses. But really, really bright light. And I felt warm and calm. And when they dug me out I was not only alive, I was in perfectly good condition except some large bruises on my back and thighs where I had hit something solid. They had no idea how I had survived but there I was. No need for C.P.R. or anything.'

'Was it just those two times?'

'Yes. Just the twice.'

'Tell me what happened on the plane again. You said someone said there was another jet.'

'Yes but I didn't see it.'

'When you found that unusual child in the desert did anything else happen to you?'

'No lights, if that is what you mean. They hit me with something and it was unbelievably scary. I was totally paralyzed and I knew they were going to do it to me again and if they did I was a goner.'

'I am going to ask you something else now and I want you to answer without thinking. What is the most important thing to you?'

'Jemma.'

'And what means the most to you after her?'

'My life is math. Lucas numbers. Sophie Germain primes. Jemma and I were looking at public key encryption together. Hey. Is that what this is about? Cryptography? Have I stumbled into some spy shit? Because it was harmless. It was just academic, I mean we had absolutely no thought of applying it or even…'

'No it's not "spy shit" in that sense.'

'Is Jemma safe? Is she OK?'

'I have no reason to believe otherwise.'

'Does she know where I am?'

'No'

'Can't you tell her? At least let her know I'm OK?'

'You are not O.K. Mike. You are in very great danger.'

'Danger of what?'

'Tell me about your interest in Lucas numbers.'

'Oh Jesus. OK. You've heard of the Fibonacci sequence?'

The man in white nodded.

'Lucas numbers and Fibonacci numbers are related. They form complementary instances of Lucas sequences. Fibonacci starts at zero. Lucas numbers work in a similar way but we start from two and one instead of zero and one so the pattern is two, one, three, four, seven, eleven, eighteen and so on. I have been looking at them and their factors and phi, the golden ratio, for a very long time. The thing that has always intrigued me is the way they come up in nature. Fibonacci numbers come up all over the place: the interlaced spirals in the seed head of a sunflower, and innumerable other examples, not just in botany but in physics too.'

Mike found himself talking with the brake off.

'Take a dish of water, add drops of oil at a set rate, run a current through it and you can use Fibonacci to accurately predict where the droplets will form patterns on the surface. Where the Fibonacci rule doesn't work, you find that Lucas numbers work. Genetics and physics are bound together. And the underlying rules they follow are universal. Everything from plant cells to salt crystals follows the rules and if you were the other side of the cosmos the same rules would apply. Absolutely the same rules. It would not matter if the life form you were looking at were not based on D.N.A.

and were entirely alien, its "design" would follow Fibonacci-Lucas numcrology.'

'Universal?'

'Yes.'

'And where did this "interest" come from.'

'I guess you'd call it a flash of inspiration,' said Mike. 'A blinding revelation, when I was at school.'

'When you were about fifteen?'

Mike's jaw swung open.

'Those lights you saw were a medium for opening up pathways in your brain, in your mind, that have shaped your thinking ever since. Woven into your experience and intuition is the key to mankind's survival. If you lose the key, you lose the world. You have to remember that Mike. When you saved that child, you bought yourself time. All knowledge is neutral. It is neither good nor bad; only what you do with it has any moral outcome or value. The ideas that you have and the direction you have been taking them in, are of immense importance to us but they are also a danger to others. You are going to be held here Mike. I have no control over that and even if I did I would not be allowed to intercede. Your instinct to save that child has saved your life but they don't know what you've seen or how far your thinking has developed and they don't like that. I can delay this for a while but they are wiping your memory. The pathways will still be there but they'll be closed. Soon, they'll seal up those pathways and throw away the key completely and forever. You'll forget about Lucas numbers and Jemma and even your name – unless you can find a way to remember, a way to hide the key from them and then find it again.'

'How? How can I possibly do that?'

'You have to find a way.'

Chapter Ten
Underground Nest

Las Vegas, NV. 1958

Colonel Philip Corso remained of the firm opinion that Eisenhower had conceded a humiliating surrender to the aliens, a capitulation made all the worse for the treaty breaches they were guilty of now. They had a new set of demands that was even viler, knowing that we could not fight them and that disclosure was impossible. The aliens were demanding that a supply of human beings for their tests. Majestic was to hand over thousands of American citizens for experimentation. And yet, Smith still seemed incapable of getting them to honor the agreement on technology transfer, and there were concerns that we might not even be dealing with the same race.

The aliens had begun by 'flirting' with aircraft and hanging around airfields before coyly disappearing. What had attracted them? Was it our technology? Perhaps when we first started beaming radio signals across the airwaves or began to take to the air at speeds only possible with jet engines or when we entered the age of atomic weaponry. The A-bomb certainly had something to do with it. Their excuse, it appeared, for not coming through with the technology transfers they promised, was that they were worried that humans would turn the alien know-how into a weapon and use it against them. Which is exactly what Corso thought they should do.

Truman had set up the C.I.A. almost as soon as the term 'flying saucer' had been coined, and only a matter of weeks after the incident at Roswell. And yet, the lack of any useful analysis or material from that 'accident' was a disaster. The question in both Corso and Smith's minds was how to deal with creatures they simply did not understand? Smith favoured negotiation but reported a shift each time they met. At first he took it for clarification; after all, they were talking through an interpreter – a machine. But it was more than that. They were pushing, like brats, to see what they could get away with and Smith had very little to push back with. They shared the lurking suspicion that they had interfered with weapons tests. There were too many damn problems for the tests to be completely free of intervention, either human or alien. Human intervention in the form of sabotage or the plain ineptitude of the rocket scientists and physicists was no more comforting to either than the alien hypothesis. Almost as if it were part of the collective consciousness, this concern was so widespread that even Douglas MacArthur – a maverick egoist emphatically not recruited to Majestic – also seemed to agree. MacArthur had developed a habit of predicting a war of the worlds between a united humanity and sinister aliens – without being aware that such a possibility existed in fact.

It had always been and remained policy to shroud

the whole issue of aliens and flying saucers in an admixture of myth and imaginary happenings. The National Security Act of 1947, which established the C.I.A., also presaged Project Sign, the first official investigation into alien technology. When that had proved a dead end, Hoyt Vandenberg demanded the Air Force come up with a prescription for all publicly acknowledged U.F.O. reports that would contain them as misidentification of the ordinary, or hoaxes. This was Project Blue Book. Hillenkoetter and his navy classmate Donald Keyhoe had been doing a swell job of muddying the water through the National Investigations Committee On Aerial Phenomena for a couple of years now. The trouble was that the aliens had moved on from hanging around over airbases to loitering near bombing ranges and tests sites. Even assuming they were just there for the fireworks – and that would be a hell of an assumption – sooner or later the Soviets would find a way of disguising their MIG jets as alien scout craft or similar. With thousands of sightings, U.F.O. reports were becoming commonplace, unremarkable even, in areas where security was a total priority. Collecting all the reports, hundreds of them, through Project Blue Book was a masterstroke. There were so many heaped in there that the relatively small number of genuine sightings were impossible to discern.

Hillenkoetter had not been able to survive the C.I.A.'s failure to predict not only the Soviet's first A-bomb test but also North Korea's invasion of the south. He remained a Majestic but was forced to pass the baton to Dulles, who, in turn, directed the agency to pursue its own research into mind control: Project MKUltra. The up-side was that there was no shortage of unwitting human guinea pigs for the mind-altering chemicals the C.I.A. tested; negroes, Hispanics, prostitutes, the insane, prisoners, soldiers and, at times, the agency's more troublesome employees. Troops at the Edgewood Arsenal in Maryland had been given mind-bending drugs: L.S.D, dope, heroin, cocaine, mescaline. The works. Some had been hypnotized. The agency had tried Chinese brainwashing techniques brought back from Korea. One poor bastard had been forced to listen to the same message over and over for more than a hundred days. Corso seriously wondered whether Dulles might have spiked the Vice-President's late night booze with one of his MKUltra chemicals. Nixon was unbalanced and could not be trusted with any Majestic information although he dropped hints occasionally that he knew 'what was happening'. Maybe he did. Maybe he was just nuts. The aim remained to find a reversible means of mind control but it generally just screwed 'subjects' up and the results were nowhere close to what the aliens achieved in a short time: almost total loss of memory and a kind of beatific afterglow, despite obvious signs of physical interference. The alien demand for humans to 'examine' had been outstripped by their propensity for abducting them and although they claimed they would do no harm there was a disturbing sexual element to their investigations. The bizarre response from the C.I.A., had been for its veterinarians to carry out random eviscerations and bodged hysterectomies on cattle; they were so crude and sadistic only a human could have been responsible. Hence anyone returned to Earth after an invasive alien experiment would be treated as the victim of a sex crime and shunned. To Corso, that kind of screwy logic was not the answer. But what tipped his hand was that on October 30, 1958, the day Ike's unilateral test ban came into force, Smith received another demand from the aliens. This time, Majestic was forced to offer them vast tracts of land under New Mexico, Colorado, Utah and Arizona: all sovereign American land, a subterranean fiefdom the size of a European country.

Operation Hardtack II promised a spectacle that could never be repeated. In the run-up to the test ban there would be flurry of nuclear explosions; twenty-nine in all, with four planned for the last day. As Douglas Reeder looked out towards the Nevada test, he reflected on the irony that the tests were so well advertised that their only novelty lay in their number. Sure, they were probably some new kind of bomb. The idea that one set of tests had been codenamed Newsreel brought a wry smile to his lips as he tugged on a Lucky Strike. A quarter of a million people died when two bombs were exploded over Hiroshima and Nagasaki in August 1945. It transpired that there were two forms of nuclear radiation: fallout from the nuclear material, some of which landed as black rain while the rest was blown away by the wind, and neutron activation, which contaminates other non-nuclear materials. There were lingering effects, including leukemia and other mutant diseases to plague the 'lucky' ones who survived. The Lord only knew what the bomb had done to the children and the unborn. And yet, by the spring of 1946, when Reeder had filed his story from Hiroshima, oleanders bloomed among the ruins. Now, a dozen years later, mushroom clouds were a tourist magnet in Las Vegas. There was a big crowd in town: family men, matrons, youngsters from the suburbs and kids from the ocean, hoods and hookers.

At nine in the evening, Smith met Dulles and Hillenkoetter at the Desert Inn. The three men had history. Dulles had co-authored the report on the C.I.A. that made Truman sack Hillenkoetter and replace him with Smith. Smith recruited Dulles to oversee the C.I.A.'s covert operations. When Smith was shifted to the Department of State Dulles became D.C.I., gaining the summit of the intelligence hierarchy. Dulles and his deputy director for plans, Richard Bissell, organized the 1953 coup in Guatemala. This led nicely the following year to Smith taking up a position at the United Fruit Company along with posts at Associated Missiles, A.M.F. Atomics, American Machine and Foundry and R.C.A. and Corning, all of which were both lucrative and, as it happened, useful to Majestic.

The three had each been instructed to 'meet me at the Sky Room', a kind of look-out tower with glass on three sides and a ceiling that sparkled with tiny lights like stars. It offered views out over the figure eight pool and the golf course. Below them, in the new gardens, older couples danced and kids lined up, young men on one side, girls opposite, to do the Stroll. Sounds drifted up from the Painted Desert Room where Art Johnson was warming up the crowd for Jimmy Durante. For piquancy, a fulsome young woman in a 'Bikini' posed at his side but the real show would take place sixty-five miles away at midnight, four hours earlier than usual, to beat the test ban. It was hard to judge the number of guests but Smith knew there were more than sixty staff in the casino itself and maybe four hundred in total, including at least two dozen local cops, paid for by the house. Floor bosses watched over the dice, blackjack and the roulette whose dealers wore pristine white shirts and stood on carpet woven with horseshoes and four-leaf clovers. Smith was unusually ebullient and, apparently in the mood to celebrate. He ordered a round of Atomic Cocktails. His upbeat air was at odds with what the others knew. The 'talks' were getting nowhere. The trio's 'associates' wanted more and more and were giving nothing. All three men were of the view that they were a royal pain in the ass; the worst kind of unwanted guests. But now there appeared to be a solution in the form of two new alliances, both of which would have to be kept their secret.

Dulles scanned the room: a confection of pink and green: gelato colors he remembered from his time in Italy. The Fascists had a sweet tooth. Even at this distance, the music from the Painted Desert showroom was still loud enough to render eavesdropping impossible. Outside, the 'Dancing Waters' of the figure-eight pool rose and fell to more music, lit by colored lights. Beyond that was Wilbur's folly, the 165-acre golf course the D.I's first owner had built despite everyone's advice, to prove anything was possible.

'Gentlemen,' said Smith. 'Let's start with some housekeeping. It looks very unlikely that we can persuade our unwanted guests to leave. The solution I propose is to find them somewhere else to stay. The moratorium of atmospheric testing will work to our advantage. I have it on reliable authority, people we can trust, that we will be able to carry out massive, simultaneous nuclear detonations to excavate suitable accommodation and facilities. This will not be cheap but we have no choice if we are to contain this problem. They have told me, and I have no reason to doubt them, that many more are on their way. I do not believe this is an armada, an invasion fleet. I believe they are dealing with a catastrophe on their own planet and need another home. Our best course of action is to provide them with what they need but to do so in such a way that they keep themselves apart and remain docile. Better to feed him than have him feed on you. It can be done, but its needs to be covert. We have to assume that very large numbers are required to create a viable colony. Our people are not ready to live side by side with them. Nor, do I think, are they willing to coexist with us.'

'Who are you proposing to build these bunkers?' said Hillenkoetter. 'Not the Army?'

'We can use the Army to construct some of the facilities. We have a genuine and increasing need for safe underground facilities to protect the President,' said Dulles. 'After all, the joint chiefs of staff have already approved the North American Air Defense Command and we are recommending a budget of around five and one half billion dollars for the Sage early warning system, more Nike Zeus rockets and so on. We can easily double that, without arousing suspicion, and if we compartmentalize adequately we can use civilian contractors for the heavy lifting. If you look around you there is construction going on at a hell of a rate. Any activity we require can be disguised and accounted for by growth in Las Vegas.'

'The people that run this town are all wops and kikes,' spat Hillenkoetter.

'They're businessmen... And the beauty of it is they are not very good businessmen.'

'Say again?' said Hillenkoetter.

'They can extort money but they can't hold on to it. A guy at the F.B.I., told me when Bugsy Seigel muscled in on the Flamingo it should've cost a million dollars to build but ended up costing six times as much. And it was half built when he stole it from Billy Wilkerson. We would hold the purse strings but their involvement would guarantee that any funds we had to use outside our own black budget would be written off as graft. They're skimming about a million dollars a day from the strip and even with all the building, the constructors are in a slump; the State Tax Commission says contractors are owed around five million in unpaid bills.'

'I wouldn't be so sure,' said Dulles.

'No-one is going to have the cojones to get too close. They have a code of silence and a system for enforcing it that makes ours look like a sieve,' said Smith. 'And they won't ask us any questions as long money comes their way.'

Smith saw a small man with slicked silver hair and a sharp suit talking with another slight figure they all recognized. The pair were shaking hands and laughing. 'Isn't that Frank Sinatra?' said Dulles. 'Is he singing tonight?' The two men parted and the silver-haired one headed towards them. 'Gentlemen,' said Smith. 'I would like you to meet Mister John Rosselli, a man of influence in Las Vegas.' They shook hands. 'Mister Roselli has a great deal of experience with construction in this part of the world. He oversaw the creation of the Tropicana, which, I understand, cost in the region of fifty million.'

'Handsome Johnny' Roselli had a bounce to his step, like a boxer light on his toes. And so he should. As a trusted man of the outfit's consiglieri, he knew that sooner or later he would be in sole charge of Up and Atom City, a town with eight million visitors a year, all of them unwittingly setting out to prove Bugsy Siegel's theorem: there ain't no lucky gamblers just winners and losers; mostly losers. His business card simply read Strategist. And for now he was content to wait for his chance to take over from the Caifano, the man with the blowtorch. The guy would burn himself one day.

Roselli also knew that this guy Dulles was a fed, but that was O.K.. There were feds and there were feds. There was the F.B.I. – the Gestapo led by a faggot whacko – and there were the defense guys who had done a fine trade in pipes and lumber when Bugsy was getting the Flamingo going. Them and good old Senator Pat McCarran, who fixed it so they could get the copper and tiles they needed. He guessed the other two guys were businessmen or maybe politicians. There was always business to be done on the golf course or in the steam room. Or in this case…

'Would you gentlemen care to join me at my table?' said Roselli with a courtly gesture. Already at the table were Morris Shenker, the mob attorney and co-owner of the Dunes, and Reeder. Dulles was happy to meet with Shenker, who he knew was also Jimmy Hoffer's lawyer – the Teamsters would have to play a big part in any construction scheme that involved moving large amounts of material around the country, and the Teamsters Central States Pension Fund had been the source of Roselli's construction funding. He was less reassured to see Reeder, who still had a reputation for digging out a good story even though he had moved off the Washington beat some years before.

Reeder recognized the intelligence trio but showed not a glimmer of surprise. Dulles saw he was a pretty shrewd poker player. 'Douglas,' said Dulles holding out a hand. If Reeder was on a story it would be about Roselli or maybe someone further up the organization, 'Joe Batters' Accardo, maybe, or his representative on Earth, Sam Giancana. He could not possibly have known the three Majestics would have been there that night. And he would have had even less idea in what capacity.

'Good to see you again, Allen,' said Reeder. 'Is this some sort of convention?'

'No,' laughed Dulles, puffing on his pipe. 'We're here to see the show.'

'The test?'

'Tests, plural. And they will be the last of their kind so we thought we'd see them in style.'

'They sure will. Can you make an official comment?'

'You know the rules.'

'Sure I do. But you can't blame me for trying,' said Reeder. 'And, thanks for the hospitality Johnny but I'll pass on your offer. Mister Roselli and the Monte Presser Talent Agency are moving into television – a very far-sighted move, if I may say so – but I prefer the coast,' he explained. 'Now, I guess I'd better find my crew before they're lured into penury.'

When Reeder had departed, making a mental note to look further into the arrival of three intelligence chiefs at the Desert Inn, Smith began the negotiations. The teamsters would be brought on board; the money would be laundered through the casinos, and the I.R.S. would stay off the mob's back. As long as no-one ever mentioned a connection to the government the outfit would skim a suitably massive profit. The discussions went on until just before midnight when the music stopped and the casino crowd moved outside, waiting with tight-throated anticipation for night to turn to day, not once but four times.

Chapter Eleven
Just Business

Alamogordo, NM. October 1958

Smith's negotiations with the new race of aliens went surprisingly well. These Tall Whites, as he began to call them, were less disturbing to look at. They looked more human, or less alien. One or the other. They were about six feet tall with proper faces – over-sized blue eyes, a proper nose, mouth and ears – and had hair, platinum blond, worn short. He could recognize individuals. In the dark, they could pass for scrawny teenagers from the prairies. They included what Smith assumed were males and females in the first group that he dealt with. And they used the same means of communication the gray aliens used, the glass tray, only they seemed to have a wider vocabulary and the voice it emitted was more like an American's.

The Tall Whites were traders. They travelled continuously and over vast distances for commerce. They told Smith that the Grays were outcasts who could not be trusted. It figured. The Earth was being used as a dumping ground, maybe even a prison. King James had sent convicts and rebels to the Americas; they might have been recast as Pilgrims but it did not turn out well for the natives, who began by feeding them. So these Tall Whites were traders? What would they trade? Had the Grays promised technology? asked the Tall White emissary. Had they delivered? How could they? The technology they promised belonged to another species, many other species from other planets. It was not theirs to give. The Tall Whites had agreements and, they said, they kept them. They would transfer technologies beginning with one that would be of mutual benefit. Earth would provide the materials and the processing required to create the form of propulsion that enabled the Tall Whites to move around the galaxy. The Earth would get to keep the technology and depending on how things worked out humans would be shown how to use it. Could the processing technology be housed underground? asked Smith. Certainly, said the emissary. And how would trade be done? We will visit, restore ourselves and move on. We will return and trade again, said the Tall White emissary. Will you leave us in peace, asked Smith. Of course, said the Tall White. Will you treat us the same? Of course, said Smith.

Chapter Twelve

Broken Lance

Washington. DC. 1960

For all that Richard Mervin Bissell PhD reminded folk of the lugubrious cartoon character Droopy, Eisenhower had regarded him as a man of action and put him in charge of the U-2 spy plane tests at Area 51. Dulles also approved of him, which is why he put him at the head of black operations including Operation 40, whose activities included destroying La Coubre, a French ship carrying Belgian ordnance in Havana harbour. It blew, killing and injuring two hundred seventy five people and taking its huge arsenal with them. Che Guevara tended the wounded; Castro pointed the finger at the U.S.A. Such was Bissell's demeanour that no-one knew whether he had been brought low by the operation's failure or thought it a success but as he shambled dejectedly into the meeting with Bob Maheu, formerly of the F.B.I., the latter was filled with foreboding. Bissell apprised him of the mission.

'Bob, I want you to kill Castro.'

'O.K.'

'Here's how you're going to do it.'

'O.K.'

'You're going to contact a man named Johnny Roselli. We know him. He will be expecting to hear from you. Roselli represents the West Coast syndicate. It has links through Las Vegas and Miami to Havana. They will carry out the work. They're pissed with Castro for shutting down the casinos and the brothels. You will represent business interests who are also pissed at Castro for nationalizing their interests in Cuba. Esso, Coca-Cola, Sears-Roebuck. No need to be specific. It's a cut-out. In the event of discovery, we will disavow any knowledge of you or the mission. A special fund has been made available for expenses. Try not to spend it.'

'O.K.'

'Any questions?'

'Nope.'

Any questions Mahue might have had were answered by Roselli's boss, who was introduced to him at the Fontainebleau Hotel in Miami Beach as Sam Flood. 'Giancana told Mahue bullets were out. It would have to be poison, so Mahue came back to us,' said Dulles. 'We went to our boys to see what they had in their locker. They have something that induces a heart attack but is untraceable. The long and the short of it was that it was SNAFU. The hit was arranged by Santo Trafficante in Miami using some local guy who turned chicken and funked it and that's why Castro is here in New York, alive and well and consorting with the likes of Malcolm X and the Brotherhood of Islam.'

Ike stood with his back to Dulles. 'Dear God,' he sighed. "Did you hear his speech at the U.N? Four and a half hours. The man is unstoppable.'

A lazy wind blew through Washington the day of John F. Kennedy's inauguration. It was too idle to go round Eisenhower so it went right through him. Washington's inauguration had been in April. Why had that tradition not been kept? He shuddered as the young whipper-snapper rose to the podium – but not only from the cold. The boy gave a good speech but goddamit he had won against his man Nixon by spending money like a sailor on liberty, and lying about a Soviet missile advantage Ike knew damn well did not exist. That money came from his Nazi-loving father's bootlegging. Old Joe Kennedy had bought that election as sure as he had supped with that other devil McCarthy. They must both have had had a long spoon. And there was Harry Truman. By God, it was almost good to see him, in comparison. Nevertheless, Kennedy would have to be told the truth and much as it would fill Ike's heart with joy to see him founder, he could not in all good faith let him drag their country down with him. More than the country: the whole human race.

The two presidents met at Eisenhower's home in Gettysburg. Mamie answered the door and saw the Secret Service into the kitchen while the men talked.

Kennedy sat stiffly, balancing a coffee on his knee. He had filled out but he was still a good-looking man. Even Mamie had, irritatingly, remarked on it. Ike felt bad that he had countered with an off-color remark about Mrs. Kennedy. But, there: it was done.

Kennedy broke the silence. 'I appreciate your

invitation, aah, Mister President. And any advice you can offer a young man.'

'Thank you, Mister President,' said Ike. 'I would not presume to tell you how to approach your office or policy. I am out of that game now and looking forward to a quiet life. But as a former military man,' he said, pulling rank on the quondam torpedo boat commander, 'the best advice I can give you is to prioritize intelligence. I don't mean your brains. You are smart enough and you have your brother with you to share the burden if the need arises. I mean the intelligence agencies.'

'I have been briefed, of course. Guatemala. Cuba. Germany.'

'Yes, of course and many times by now, no doubt. But I have to tell you that when I received my first briefing, I did not hear much that I didn't know already. It's not what they tell you, it's what they hide – what they keep occult.'

Kennedy shifted in his seat. 'Occult?'

'You must assert your authority over the agencies. In particular: covert operations and their budgets. I know you do not share my views on the need for holding a tight rein but you will need to keep account of what is being spent in the name of defense.'

'I plan to get this country moving. Defense spending is one means. We will not stint in our efforts to counter the Soviet threat or efforts to undermine our democracy through espionage or any other means.'

'And space?'

'Space is another. The Soviet program is a threat to the U.S.A. both militarily and in terms of the nation's morale. I am determined that we shall not only close the gap in technology between the U.S.A. and the Soviets but that we will take the lead with Project Mercury. It is well advanced and I intend to see that it is properly funded.'

'N.A.S.A. is doing a fine job but I do not believe that all the opportunities for technological advance are being taken advantage of. I would advise you to pay close attention to the role the intelligence agencies are playing.'

'The C.I.A. is rightly chastened by the loss of the U2 last year and the capture of Gary Powers. We are making every effort to secure his release.'

Ike held back from saying that Powers might not be in a Russian dungeon if the missile gap with the Soviets had not been exaggerated. Neil McElroy had been spooked by the launch of Sputnik-1 just a month after he had become Secretary of State for Defense and that had been enough to skew the intel on the Soviets' I.C.B.M. missile program. To its credit the C.I.A. had been less like Chicken Little than the Air Force, but the uncertainty had persuaded Ike to authorize a U-2 mission over the U.S.S.R. in 1959 for the first time in 16 months. It had proved nothing and had to be followed up, and that was when Powers had been shot down.

'What do you know about the budget for the U2?' Ike asked Kennedy.

'I don't have the figures to hand.'

'McElroy and I kept the official defense budget down to about forty billion but that is a drop in the bucket,' Ike said, allowing a moment for Kennedy to feel the full weight of what he was saying. 'Under the C.I.A. Act, the D.C.I. has the power to spend unvouchered money. Basically, Harry Truman gave him carte blanche. And I don't believe he is properly accountable. I do not believe that I was receiving all the information I was due. And I do not believe that the agency and associated covert committees are sharing hard-won advances in technology to the extent that would be required of true patriots. Furthermore, some people, some corporations, are going to get very rich out of the present situation and they will not all be acting in the nation's best interests. They are profiteering and worse.'

'This is the military industrial complex you described in your farewell address?' said Kennedy. '"In the councils of government, we must guard against the acquisition of unwarranted influence, whether sought or unsought, by the military-industrial complex. The potential for the disastrous rise of misplaced power exists, and will persist. We must never let the weight of this combination endanger our liberties or democratic processes."'

'That is one aspect of it,' Eisenhower agreed, flattered that the young man should have committed the speech to memory. 'But not all. Had I been able to be totally honest with the American public I would have added in another term. When you talk to Beetle Smith and Allen Dulles you will need to ask them about our space budget and what is really going on. I had to make some very far-reaching decisions and I pity you my boy, because you will have to pay for them.'

'Sir, if the C.I.A. is over-reaching its authority, and it is hiding expenses or its activities from the President I shall ensure that it is smashed into a thousand pieces and scattered to the winds.'

Why couldn't he just come out with it? The whole damned alien business. Ike cursed his own vanity and the fear of losing his place in history as the man who won World War Two and going down forever as the man who sold humanity's birthright. His own failure to be forthright disgusted Ike but perhaps Kennedy would have the wit to piece together the coded message in his farewell speech and the hints he had just dropped. And maybe he could make a better fist of dealing with the aliens, and Majestic, than Ike feared he had. Ike's heart had been failing since fifty-five; it was only a question of time before the chariot race in his chest was lost. Que sera, sera.

When they parted, Ike could see Kennedy had questions.

Jack Kennedy winced as he reached for the file on the Resolute Desk, which Jacquie had returned to its rightful place in the Oval Office. Stretching for the file sent a clap of pain through his left hip, that he knew would resonate for an hour or more even dosed with codeine and Demerol. Johnson recognized the signs. He and House Speaker Sam Rayburn had used the knowledge that J.F.K. was a sick man to pressure him into accepting the Texan as his running mate. Kennedy had not forgotten either, but Johnson had proved a good man in a fight and even Bobby, who hated Johnson's guts, had reluctantly begun to accept that he was, in fact, loyal. Johnson had told Dulles that 'if he was a horse I'd shoot him myself,' but, if anything, he had come to respect the President's ability to function under the combined influences of methadone, Librium, barbiturates, antihistamines and shots for his thyroid and colitis. 'And Eli Lilly would pay for the funeral.'

Jack had also needed Johnson to gain the support of the Southern Democrats, plus as a leader of the House he had had a lot of pull. Very few could resist the Johnson treatment, hours of wheedling and pummeling, Johnson towering over his target with his face inches away, every doubt anticipated and shot down, every argument destroyed. Joe Kennedy had wanted Jack to do a deal with L.B.J. Bobby had done his best to torpedo the hastily arranged partnership but in the end both brothers knew the nomination would be a near thing and every vote counted.

Later they would form even more dubious alliances, via Joe Kennedy and his links to the mafia and to the teamsters: an obligation Bobby, especially, felt like a rock around his neck. Bobby, as attorney general, was keen to put distance between the White House and the likes of Sam Giancana and his go-between, Sinatra, because of, rather than despite, their help in winning Jack the West Virginia Primary and the crucial votes in Illinois.

Jack could not care less. He had not wanted his little brother in the role, and he liked Sinatra. Sinatra had introduced him to Judith Campbell, who among other talents had found a way to ease Jack's pain, literally, if only for the duration of sex. His osteoporosis and a painful priapism both responded to treatment with a frequency that Jack felt unable, decently, to request from Jacquie. Although they weren't aware of the cause, the boys in the Secret Service knew of the effect and had given Jack the codename Lancer. Joe, meanwhile, had cooled on Sinatra after he had introduced Jack and Sam Giancana directly – a dumb move by the 'wop lickspittle' – plus he hung around with Sammie Davies Jr. who wasn't just black but compounded the felony by being a Jew. Joseph Senior had standards for his remaining sons.

Now that Jack was elected and Bobby appointed, the main problem they both had with Lyndon Johnson was that he had the ear of the press and he couldn't sit still. The first thing Jack had had to do was to find Johnson something to keep him busy. He had tried letting him sit in on National Security Council meetings and put him in charge of an ad hoc committee on science. But he couldn't help but butt in. Today, the Soviets had put a man in space. They had had no foreknowledge of how he would cope in zero gravity or whether the first cosmonaut would burn to death. Firing Yuri Gagarin out of the atmosphere was like a huge, uncontrolled circus act, but his one hundred eight-minute torment ended when he broke free of his red-hot capsule and parachuted to safety. The capsule smashed into the desert floor and covered America's face with egg. Its man, Alan Shepard, had been training for a sub-orbital flight on a Mercury-Redstone rocket slated for just a month later. Now the U.S.A would always be number two in space. Here was a real test for Johnson.

'I ahh, spoke with President Eisenhower shortly after my inauguration and ahh we discussed the issue of space and ahh other matters,' said Kennedy. Johnson paced, as he had ever since he quit his sixty a day habit. 'What is your assessment as chairman of the National Aeronautics Space Council of the news today?'

'It is four years since the Soviets sent a dog into space. That muttnik died up there but I guess it was only a matter of time before they sent one of their own up, even a juvenile midget.'

'A midget?'

'Almost a monkey. Five feet two,' drawled the six foot four Johnson.

'Putting a man into orbit and bringing him safely down to Earth ahh emphasizes the disparity that exists between Soviet capabilities and our own. How long will it be before they can pilot a weapon that can be directed from space on to the United States or simply send up a missile that will fly too high to be detected?'

'I have no idea. But what I do know is we need to find a way to whip their Slavic asses. If they can put a man in space, we should put a man on the moon.'

'Is that physically possible?'

'It'd be like shooting a can of meat across the Pacific, but, sure, it's possible. Getting the poor bastard back'd be the hard part.'

'Find a way.'

There was a knock at the door. 'The Director of Central Intelligence,' said an aide.

'Send him in,' said Kennedy.

Dulles entered with Bissell. They were both still smarting from Kennedy's Executive Order 10920 in February, which abolished the Operations Coordinating Board responsible for psych war and handed its responsibilities over to national security advisor, McGeorge Bundy, and the Department of State. Dulles was particularly sore. First, it was a sign Kennedy wanted control over the program, which was on his turf. Second, it potentially exposed MKUltra and, third, that meant Majestic. Given Kennedy's connections and the nature of the construction program, like him or not, the President was, without knowing it, walking into a minefield. He had to be protected against himself. There was also a great deal more at stake now for Majestic and no elected official could be allowed to interfere with its mission. But for the moment, the topic was the invasion of Cuba. Kennedy's support was half-hearted to say the least. He had to be put in a position to back it fully, to commit U.S. troops if, or when, the invasion force failed to hook up with the guerrillas in the Escambray Mountains. He still could not read Kennedy and that was a damn curse. Worse was to come for Dulles. The invasion was a fiasco. Kennedy had not risen to the bait. He refused to commit U.S. troops and actually cut the air support Bissell needed. The Brigade's route had been blocked by twenty thousand Cuban troops and within seventy-two hours the invaders had all been killed or had surrendered. Dulles was hanging in there but Bissell was on his way out.

But later, Dulles confided to Smith that there was 'light on the horizon. Since Gagarin went into orbit, Kennedy has become obsessed with space. His speech to Congress asking for nine billion dollars to send a man to the moon before the end of the decade means we'll have more latitude to develop our new technologies faster than we thought. The black budget and our scope for using contractors will rise accordingly.'

'You know, we're going to have to think about patents. I have no objection to owning some.'

'Me either. We can get people working on that. We just need to ensure that the whole operation is broken down into as many parts as possible and that no one person or group knows what anyone else in the network is doing.'

'Need to know,' nodded Smith. 'Very good. The Tall White aliens are traders. They'll provide anything that they can see a profit in and so far they have been utterly true to their word.'

'Unlike the Grays.'

'Unlike the Grays,' agreed Smith. 'We now have two programs running: one to build bunkers for the Grays, while we still can't risk cleaning them out, and a second project to supply the needs of the Tall Whites. It is not clear what we're building for them but it appears to be a refinery of sorts. There is the risk that we are building our own means of destruction but our engineers say everything we've created so far has been reversible.'

'Whatever comes our way, the development work can be ascribed to the space program.'

Smith nodded. 'The Grays, on the other hand, are just voracious. We agreed they would provide a way of keeping tabs on who they were taking but it is running into thousands. I really do not know where it is going to stop. Our best hope lies in the fact that there is clear animosity towards them from the Tall Whites, who seem to find them as disgusting as we do. It's very clear that we have to keep the facilities for both well apart. We need to keep the Grays segregated under new Mexico and find a better way of hiding the Tall Whites' comings and goings in Nevada.'

'Maybe they could help with that. They must have the technology and it would be in their interest to use it.'

'That makes it even more essential that we keep this out of public view and certainly away from the president.'

'That's going to be difficult,' said Corso, joining them. 'Take a look at this.'

'What is it?' asked Dulles.

'It's the draft of a National Security Memorandum, which the President will send to the joint chiefs of staff, demanding a review of all psych war activities – including anything U.F.O-related.'

'How did you get this?' gasped Smith.

'We have to lock Majestic down tight. We can't trust the President,' snarled Dulles. 'Under no circumstances should we disclose anything related to Majestic, the Grays or the Tall Whites. All black activities, budget, construction, exploitation, anything at all. Not to Kennedy. Not to the national security staff.'

Smith found each meeting with the Grays less and less fruitful and more frustrating. The Tall Whites were warier and took some coaxing but, if they could be described that way, they were also more polite, as long, that is, as you moved slowly, talked quietly and avoided any kind of ambiguity in your dealings with them. Like the Grays, they had a disquieting habit of conferring at a frequency above or below human hearing, which made it seem like they were using telepathy but they also appeared to check themselves, as if they realised they were being rude. It was almost charming. The Grays also spoke inaudibly to one another but would drop into a hiss like the white noise from a transistor radio. The worst of their kind, assuming they were of their kind, were the taller long-nosed variety. They carried a definite air of menace.

The Majestic scientists had suggested these taller Grays were adults or perhaps adolescents, while the shorter ones were at some earlier stage of development. It might explain why they were such bad pilots. To get half way across the universe and then crash in a field took some doing. Or maybe it was the design of the craft they flew. After all they were made to fly outside an atmosphere. The nature of the few shards the Air Force had collected from alien crash sites remained a mystery. At first glance they appeared metallic but a closer look showed they were opalescent and laminar in construction. The nearest Earth equivalent would be mother-of-pearl.

Both species seemed to share the same form of propulsion for their vehicles though the Tall Whites' were far larger and, the Majestic scientists guessed, were designed to travel further. Getting too close to either type of vehicle was a mistake. There was some radiant heat, probably residual from the flight, but no radioactivity or E.M. radiation such as x-rays or radio, but there was something that effectively dissolved some types of plant life, mainly woody trees and vines, and bone, not only in humans but also in any poor critter that strayed too close.

The other difference was that the Grays had to land their craft and then taxi them underground at Holloman, where subterranean hangars had been built for them under the guise of creating atomic shelters. The Tall Whites at Indian Springs had some way of burying their craft like a stingray hiding on the seabed. The extraordinary thing was that they appeared to do it in solid rock but were able to come out again and fly off. The scientists' hypothesis was that that it was a form of camouflage, an illusion, perhaps caused by bending light. The military potential was obvious which might be why they were reluctant to divulge its secret. The Tall Whites seemed to operate on a very simple principle. They gave nothing for nothing. There always had to be a quid pro quo. The Grays offered plenty, demanded plenty and gave next to nothing.

As his driver steered the E-Z-go golf cart deeper along the underground passage of the New Mexico salt mine. the walls began to dry out and the heat rose. As they approached Smith's by-now habitual meeting place with the Grays, he experienced a familiar pang of distaste but nothing could have prepared him for what he saw next.

A group of the taller Grays surrounded an object on the floor. Half faced inwards, the others were formed in a defensive cluster, like circled wagons on the prairie. It was hard to see what was in their midst but it looked like a pile of fish and even from a distance of about fifteen yards it stank so bad Smith gagged.

The outward-facing Grays crouched and held out their thumb-less hands which now more closely resembled claws, and their small mouths emitted the white noise while their carapace-like eyes followed his and the driver's every, measured, move. Smith knew instinctively that this was a threat, the first they had made. Until now, they had seemed harmless, if repulsive. From the corner of his eye he could see the driver's hand moving towards his holster. 'Don't make the first move,' whispered Smith. 'Just stay calm.'

The defenders shuffled forwards leaving an inner circle whose movements were now unusually animated. At the top of the slippery mound were two halves of a Gray's body, split and empty like a walnut shell. Around it was coiled gray skin, frothing like a slug dosed with salt, and from the spume crawled a lizard-like creature that stretched and stood on its rear two legs.

The stench was unbearable. The driver doubled over and retched. The sudden movement triggered an attack by the outer circle of Grays, who pounced on him before he could pull his gun, pounding him and shoving their fingers into his eyes and mouth so that he choked in blinded agony. The others advanced on Smith, who felt an invisible grip around his chest, sending serrated agony up his neck and through his stomach, and squeezing all the air from his lungs.

Officially, Smith had died of his heart attack on the way from home to Walter Reed Army Hospital in Washington. Majestic was left without a negotiator but with a new type of alien, a new reptilian variety of Gray, to deal with. The specimen whose metamorphosis, or was it whose birth, Smith had witnessed was uncommunicative. Detlev Bronk had been drafted in temporarily to fill the gap and one of the taller Grays explained, in a roundabout way, that the others had been protecting it. Similar transformations or arrivals would, no doubt, ensue. They had no word for birth. Hyenck had a theory they were matriphages: they consumed their mothers, like some kinds of spider, shortly after 'birth'. It would be an efficient way of using resources on long interstellar journeys. He had also put forward the idea that once they had something bigger to populate than a spaceship, such as the caverns under New Mexico they might start building their numbers until they burst out and swarmed like cicadas. Bronk held both ideas at bay. And for now, he could do little more than ask questions and try to interpret the answers. Smith's absence had disturbed the Tall Whites too. It took them time to get used to a human, to trust him and Bronk suspected that if he were to introduce himself and then disappear again they might react badly, jeopardizing any further progress.

Dulles had considered Corso as a replacement for Smith but his negotiating skills were not up to the job and his antagonism towards the Grays got in the way. Not just towards the Grays either. Dulles could feel it radiating off the frog-eyed bastard each time they met. Souers had persuaded Dulles to give Gordon Cray the job. Dulles had had misgivings. He wanted Cray to spend as much time as possible as Majestic's inside man on the President's Foreign Intelligence Advisory Board, obfuscating on the subject of 'the quality and adequacy of intelligence collection, of analysis and estimates, of counterintelligence, and of other intelligence activities.' Dulles, meanwhile, would concentrate on finding a money man to handle the increasingly complicated business of round-tripping funds, setting up a secret Majestic bank, laundering money through the casinos and pay-rolling both the Gray and Tall White programs. The numbers were piling up and at some point the Treasury and the I.R.S. would surely take an interest.

Dulles had taken his eye off the ball just as Kennedy's suspicions began to coalesce. In quick succession, Kennedy issued a new National Security Memorandum, using the term MJ-12 specifically but relating it to psychological warfare again, and then began a tour of Indian Springs Air Force Base and the Nevada test site using Marine One, the presidential helicopter. He had flown dangerously close to Dog Bone Lake and even though there would be nothing for him to see from the air, the idea that he might suspect the existence of the Tall Whites unnerved Dulles. Johnson had told Dulles a further trip to Holloman A.F.B. at Almogardo, New Mexico was on the cards. Holloman was Gray-central. Dulles fed Johnson a line about radiation levels and advised him to delay the President's visit by a year at least.

When Dulles next met Kennedy it was at the C.I.A. building in Langley. Jack Kennedy looked round at the members of the agency gathered there for the ceremony and began, as he often did, by flattering the crowd. 'I want, first of all, to express my appreciation to you all for the opportunity that this ceremony gives to tell you how grateful we are in the government and in the country for the services that the personnel of this Agency render to the country,' he said. 'It is not always easy. Your successes are unheralded; your failures are trumpeted. I sometimes have that feeling myself. But I am sure you realize how important is your work, how essential it is and how, in the long sweep of history, how significant your efforts will be judged. So I do want to express my appreciation to you now, and I'm confident that in the future you will continue to merit the appreciation of our country, as you have in the past.' He praised Dulles for his modesty, unswerving purpose in office, and unprecedented public service and then presented the medal that signified that the services of Dulles, Bissell, Deputy Director Charles Cabell and a handful of others were no longer required.

As his personal secretary, Evelyn Lincoln had a clear view of the President's desk from her office, which was a stopping-off point for visitors, mostly male and of all ages. Although she idolized him, she was safe from the President's advances and those of his court. Married, of a certain age and no oil painting, Jack valued her for her unwavering efficiency, maternal ambition and absolute discretion in his personal matters, which frequently involved arranging a sexual liaison. The assorted senators, aides, supplicants and lobbyists who stopped by her desk were offered second-rate cigars from the humidor and candy from a bowl. Corso chose the latter on his first visit and presented Evelyn with an 'eyes only' folder of intelligence material on U.F.O.s to pass to the President. Kennedy had made yet another offer to the Soviets of joining forces to reach the moon. Khrushchev had apparently ignored it but the President wanted to clear any objects – including U.F.Os – out the way in case Nikita changed his mind. As she went in Corso could see Jack and Bobby were in deep discussion with a group of men he knew from the backs of their heads. They were from the I.R.S. Bobby seemed to be dominating the discussion but Corso could not tell more than that. It was not what Corso was interested in, anyway. His focus was on the T.V., which he knew the President watched when there was an event such as a launch from Cape Canaveral. He intended to bug it.

The Majestics now numbered twenty and included Maurice H. Stans, Ike's former director of the Bureau of the Budget, and Earl Warren who oversaw treaties and contracts. The money side of the business called for top brains and men who could be trusted. Dulles had voted himself chairman, or MJ-1 as he now styled himself. Corso was still very much the junior and still did not merit an MJ number but he had two pieces of news that he knew would shake things up. At Kennedy's insistence, the President and Johnson planned another visit to Holloman and Indian Springs. This time they would not be put off. When Bush had finished his report on technological progress, Corso flourished a reel of quarter-inch tape.

'My estimate is that neither Kennedy nor Johnson are aware of the existence of the aliens or of any pact,' Corso announced, wrongly. 'He is, however, extremely concerned about the cost of the Apollo program and the defense budget, hence he has made the offer of sharing the cost of reaching the moon with the Soviets. He is also proposing to sign a treaty banning nuclear weapon tests in the atmosphere, under water and, crucially, in outer space, with the Soviets and the United Kingdom.'

'He's right, of course, to worry about costs,' said Stans.

'He's selling us out to save a few bucks,' sneered Corso.

'Hardly a "few" bucks,' snorted Cray.

'He's also right to hold back money for defense,' Souers chipped in. 'There's another war in Asia coming. We tripled the number of advisors we sent to Indo-China last year and the year before,'

'The issue is not the amount of money involved. It is that we're in the process of creating an invisible, parallel economy. A second set of books,' said Stans. 'The person we have to be wary of is not the President, it's the attorney general.'

'That little ass-hole has been relentless in chasing down Hoffer and the others,' Hillenkoetter hissed. 'We need the teamsters and our other allies and he's going to screw it all up.'

Dulles looked round the table and began to sort the sheep from the goats. 'We clearly cannot permit the President to visit either base and nor can we permit our operations to be subverted by the A.G. I suggest we convene a subcommittee to look into ways to deal with the executive. Are we all agreed?' There was silence from those who understood what they were being asked and a noncommittal shrug from one or two others.

'Gordon, Corso, Admiral Hillenkoetter, I would like you stay behind. My thanks as usual to rest of you gentlemen for your time. We will meet again in December.'

The four men sat quietly for about five minutes before they sensed a common agreement. 'I take it we all concur that this is a wet situation?' asked Dulles. Each nodded in turn.

'Can we rely on outsiders?' asked Cray.

'Up to a point. We'll fix up a patsy. There's a guy – ex-Marine, Lee Oswald – we have been keeping an eye on since he came back from the Soviet Union a couple of years back. He'd be a natural fall guy. We have the use of MKUltra if we need it. But we'll need at least one of our own as back-up and when the shit hits the fan the mob can take the heat,' said Dulles.

'You've been thinking about this for a while,' said Cray.

'Yes and I have a medal to prove it,' answered

Dulles. 'We'll use one of the Secret Service guys, too.'

'There will be an inquiry.'

'We can fix that.'

'This is treason,' said Cray.

'It's our duty to humanity,' said Corso, pompously.

'You're a regular Boy Scout,' said Hillenkoetter.

'What about Bobby?'

'We'll fix him too, but Lancer is the priority.'

Everyone who was alive that day remembers Jack Kennedy's assassination. Most remember it wrong, and for a reason: Earl Warren and the other Majestics had two things to hide. First: both during the event and after, Majestic and its unwitting collaborators expended a great deal of energy and effort on developing competing conspiracy theories. They included the idea that aliens killed J.F.K., which, in effect, they had, by proxy. By comparison, even theories involving, Marilyn Monroe, 'Mooney Sam' Giancana, Castro, Kruschev, Hoover and Johnson – or all of them together – seemed plausible to the many who just couldn't come to terms with the tragedy. In the end it was all white noise. And no-one would ever know or believe the truth. Second: At the exact same time the President's motorcade turned into Elm, Corso was taking matters into his own hands.

Corso wasn't in Dallas. He was at Dulce Base in New Mexico, with an agency man called Ted Anders and a

Special Forces engineer sergeant, name of Hill, from Fort Kobbe. Reeder knew this because he had run into Anders when he was writing a story on the twenty-fifth anniversary of the 1941 Bataan Death March. Anders had survived capture by the Japanese and the two had first met ten years later as the U.S. prepared to end its occupation of the Land of the Rising Sun. Shortly after, Anders joined the C.I.A.'s Directorate of Plans, where he remained. He wanted to talk about anything except the March and he found himself gabbing about the three brothers he had lost, in particular, the eldest.

'Sam was in Okinawa with the Tenth Army,' he told Reeder. 'You heard of "blowtorch and corkscrew"? They had to fight their way up to the caves, hand-to-hand with Jap mortar fire all round. When they finally secured the area in front of the caves, they would pump a hundred gallons of gasoline into them, one at a time, and set it off with tracer bullets or phosphorus grenades. That's what they had to do. And those caves were deep.' Reeder poured another glass and wondered where this was going. 'Caves are damn near invulnerable. Let me tell you about Korea. Our intel was that the reds had whole warehouses and barracks, whole units of artillery underground but you know where they really screwed us? We would bomb the hell out of them and fire every kind of munitions into their false entrances and blank caves and they them would come out in their hordes and engage us in hand-to-hand and, by God, they overwhelmed our boys. They cut us to pieces.' Reeder waited. 'You're gonna think I've flipped but I got tell you something. We have got a goddam war going on under out feet and we're going to lose it.'

'Under our feet?'

'The day President Kennedy was shot I observed a blowtorch and corkscrew operation against – how can I put it? – against the inhabitants of the cave system under New Mexico. It warned against it but I was ignored.'

'Who the hell lives under New Mexico?'

'Not who. What,' said Anders.

A quarter of a mile down, second lieutenant Eric Brocker had been the first to actually encounter a gray alien on that operation, he said. They appeared to have retreated deeper and deeper into the system. When the soldiers doused their lamps it was the blackest dark they had ever experienced. Brocker was sure he could hear Grays scuttling away ahead of his platoon, squeaking and scratching round the next turn. As he entered a dome-like cavern he saw one lying twisted on the floor. Frothing. He looked up and his lamp caught others appended to the rocks to above, like limpets, their slippery skins glistening and their dead, scaly eyes sucking up the beam from his flashlight. The walls were like polished glass where the tunnel-bores had melted the rock. The alien must have slipped and fallen. Without thinking, Brocker grabbed it and called for a medic, who saw what he was doing and helped him carry the wounded alien from the cave, using the fabric of its clothing for grip.

It was like trying to carry a huge, half-dead fish. They could hear an agitated hissing behind. As Brocker and the medic carried the alien to the next turn, one of the platoon threw a grenade. The hissing turned to a howl that rose until it was beyond their hearing. Gray survivors writhed, and slithered away. But their retreat was blocked by other reptilian creatures, hundreds of them. It took Brocker and the medic close to an hour to reach the cave entrance. They still had the wounded Gray with them. For some reason, the other creatures had kept their distance. Brocker saw daylight and as soon as he reached it Corso screamed 'Seal it. Seal it.' And the Marines blasted the cave with flamethrowers. Anders found himself whispering, 'Father, forgive them; for they know not what they do.'

The field autopsy on the Gray revealed that its blood was copper-based and blue like a helmet crab's, hence the skin color. Its body cavity was filled with a marshmallow-like substance that appeared to function as its internal organs or possibly as a food source, and its brain, assuming that was what the organ in its head was, was no bigger than a hen's egg and resembled angel's hair pasta. Its skeleton was riddled with tiny holes like a loofer sponge and at the centre of the body there was something like a large, soft, empty turtle's egg. They wrapped the remains and put them in a cold truck and locked the doors. 'When they opened it there was one of the reptiles inside,' said Anders. 'Alive.'

Reeder did not know what to make of Anders or his story. It was so crazy he had to have water-tight, stand-up, irrefutable evidence before going public on something like that. He needed someone on the inside. Someone credible. Elsewhere, though, Cray had taken it seriously and was scared. His analysis was A) That Corso had accomplished the equivalent of poking a stick into a wasp nest and beating it around. B) That the gray aliens were massing underground just as Hyenck predicted. C) Either the reptiles were parasitoidal, hatching inside their hosts and feeding off them, or D) these aliens had the power to resurrect themselves and E) Only the Tall White aliens could deal with the Grays. He set up a meeting directly after the event with the Tall White female he had dealt with on three previous occasions. He assumed she was female; they were all oddly sexless, in Cray's opinion. She was about half a foot taller than he. Her skin had an almost ceramic quality – only her face and thumb-less hands were exposed. The fabric of her long, white robe. hung around her curve-less frame. When she moved, she glided like a well-trained geisha, although he knew that they could really shift when they wanted. Cray also knew that like others he had been seduced by a form that fit the racial ideals he shared with the other Majestics; the Tall Whites' palor, their apparent gentility and their punctiliousness in business. At heart, he also knew that his reaction was ignorance, justified. In other words, plain prejudice.

He had learned to sit quietly and passively, sometimes

for up to an hour, before attempting to converse with the female White. She seemed to respond well to that. And now he would ask: 'What would you require to help us with the gray aliens?'

The voice from the tablet responded. 'Do you mean destroy them?'

'Yes.'

'Do you want a war?'

'No'

'If you are prepared to pay, we will ensure that they stay where they are.'

'Be their jailers?'

'Their keepers.'

'You can't just get rid of them?'

'You do want a war.'

'No one wants a war. We just want to get rid of them. They're vermin.'

'We can contain them.'

'But you can't get rid of them entirely? Wipe them out?'

'We trade with them.'

'They're disgusting.'

'Yes.'

'Can you stop them swarming?'

'For now.'

'What will happen when they do swarm?'

'It is their planet.'

'This is our planet.'

'There are a million and a half species on this planet. You claimed sole title but you relinquished it.'

'But we have always been here.'

She looked at him blankly.

'The swarming,' said Cray. 'Can you at least delay that?'

'Yes.'

'For how long?'

She gave no answer.

'Is there a way of escaping from them if they swarm?'

'Yes. For some.'

'Some? Not all?'

'You, for example. And your… children.'

'What do you want in return?'

'We will make a list.'

Chapter Thirteen

Global Warming

Since revealing to him that Mike was about to have his memory wiped, the man in white had suddenly, and not a little irritatingly, become more communicative, to the point that Mike was struggling to absorb the information he was being given: the existence of alien species on Earth, the historic dealings between his government and these other beings, the attempts to eradicate them…

'The Tall Whites neutralized the Grays. Military engineers cleared them out and buried them in large pits and then waited,' the man in white told him.

'For what?' asked Mike, aware that he sounded like a kid being told a bedtime story.

'For the next generation to emerge. The parasites they carry have a kind of homing instinct. As they emerged, your soldiers would fry them with a kind or flame-throwing rocket launcher you people developed specifically for that job. They had to be quick. It had to be as soon as they came out, before they toughened up and before they started communicating with the others. Like newborn turtles. When they were all out of the pits they were incinerated, sealed in concrete and logged as nuclear waste. There's about million of them under Arizona.'

'You said the Tall White aliens were paid for this?'

'Yes.'

'What with?'

'Mainly with materials that were mined and then processed using colliders. Metals, gases. The Tall Whites did very well out of the service they provided. The costs were hidden by your Vietnam War and your Space Race.'

'Are they still doing it?'

'Sure.'

'What pays for it?'

'Drugs. Dams. Tax.'

'Drugs?'

'Majestic is everywhere Mike. People don't even know they're working for it.'

'But drugs?'

'What did you expect?'

Mike tried to get a grip, to think back over everything the man in white had told him.

'How do you know all this about Truman and Eisenhower and the Kennedys?' he asked.

'I was there,' said the man in white.

'Truman was President at the end of World War Two. That's more than seventy years ago.'

'That is correct.'

'Seventy.'

'Yes.'

'So how old are you supposed to be?'

'We don't measure our age. There's no point.'

One of us has gone nuts, thought Mike.

'You're not human?'

'No.'

'What are you?'

'It doesn't matter. Let's just say I am different.'

'You're saying you're not human,' said Mike. 'And you have been in close contact with Presidents, close enough to have an idea what they were thinking, for decades and no one has noticed?'

'That is correct.'

'So there's this guy. Who never ages and no one has ever heard about, right at the heart of government, generation after generation, and no one notices?'

'That is correct.'

'So, you're immortal, too?'

'No. We have finite existence but we don't decay like you. However, my time is nearly up.'

'Is this when you say "Only one man can save the human race."And it's me?"

'There are others Mike but you are in a special position.'

'So you said, although you didn't explain,' said Mike, wearily.

'I will.'

'You can start by telling me how you remain

invisible to the security services, secretaries, the President's cat and the world's cameras.'

'Cameras are a problem but cats can't talk to you and all the rest see what they expect to see. Have you ever heard the idea that you only use about ten percent of your brain?'

'Yes,' said Mike cautiously.

'That's all crap, Mike. Evolution does not work that way, anywhere.'

'Can I just ask something?'

'Sure.'

'Do aliens say "crap"?

'Sure. Crap.'

'Only, you don't sound like an alien.'

'No. I sound like a human. That's the idea, Mike.'

'And you look like one. Do you look like one or are you in some sort of disguise, Are you going to peel off a latex mask?'

'That's not how it works. About two thirds of your brain is there to interpret the tiny amount of information that comes through your optic nerve, and make sense of it. Human sense. Almost everything you think you see is imaginary and there are limits to your imagination, evolutionary limits created by conditions here on Earth over the course of your development as a species. Your senses developed to cope with this planet and your world. There was a lot of adaptation along the way. You think you see everything like a wide screen movie with full motion and the whole picture playing in front of you. You don't see any of that. Have you ever looked at the moon, Mike?'

'Sure I have.'

'How big is it?'

'About two thousand miles across.'

'From this distance, you can cover it with the end of thumb, when you hold your arm out, can't you?'

Mike nodded.

'That is about the amount of your vision that goes into the two per cent of your physical body weight that is your brain. It's a tiny, fragmentary snapshot, three times a second. Your eye moves randomly picking up little pieces of information and everything you see, colors, movement, shadow, shapes, faces, landscapes, all happen inside your brain. And it plays tricks on you.'

'Are you saying you do that?'

'My kind evolved to see more frequencies of light and millions more colors than you. So did a lot of species here, as it happens. It does not take much to disrupt the messages going through your visual system and you do the rest for us.'

'You're not some sort of shape-shifter?'

'More like a chameleon. Pigeons and butterflies can see me as I am, but you don't.'

'That could be a blessing.'

'The light you talked about. Remember Rendlesham and the avalanche?'

‘Was that you?’

‘No. It was purely accidental. The light you “saw” when you were young was your brain’s optical processing system overloading: a psychedelic episode. The avalanche you were trapped in triggered a flashback. Also, possibly, your experience after the air crash.’

‘I was drugged?’

‘It was literally a form of enlightenment. New neural pathways. You have now acuities that few other humans have, which is why you are important. The avalanche, your rescue and rehabilitation after the plane crash: they were for a reason. You’re a valuable asset.’

‘You’re telling me I have a superpower? You have to be kidding.’

‘Not a “superpower”, as you put it, but a raised level of consciousness. The visitors are only half your problem. As far as they’re concerned, they have balanced things out by letting you live. In itself, that is exceptional. They do not play a zero-sum game. They’re punctilious in their dealings. Once they have given their word they keep it but they only make trades that benefit them and they won’t give anything away.’

‘Who are they? Where do they come from?’

‘They’re a very old race of nomadic traders.’

‘How old?’

‘As a race. Ancient by your standards. Individually? Their lifespan is about ten times that of a human. The ones you have seen are mainly youths. They have a growth spurt towards the end of their lives. We do not know where they came from originally. We think it was in what you know as the constellation of Bootes, but they started journeying many, many generations back. Now they can use the dark matter matrix to travel, in effect, many times the speed of light. The fuel you provide will enable them to relay goods back to their nearest way-planet and take them on to the next. It was not always like that. You have to appreciate that the distances involved are vast and even traveling at close to the speed of light, it once took whole lifetimes for the Tall Whites to probe, explore, land, trade and then move on. Some of them would be born and die without seeing either end of their journey. The next generation and the ones after that have always been important to them; that is why they are so protective of their children and probably why you are being saved.'

'What do they want here?'

'The underground facilities that you found are part of a huge complex, built partly to their design. It is used to mine the particles that drive their craft. They catapult through time-space using dark energy, creating a kind of quantum lubricant, a plasma, that allows their craft to slip through dark and bright matter. It disrupts at a sub-molecular level, which is how they penetrate rock with their craft. Space is not a vacuum. You can't travel across a whole galaxy without hitting something with mass, sooner or later.'

'How does it work?'

‘Honestly? That’s as much as I know. I’m not an engineer.’

‘What are you, then?’

‘An observer. A regulator.’

‘An interstellar cop.’

‘If you like.’

‘And what do you want from us?’

‘I’m not observing you, I’m observing them, to make sure they keep to the rules.’

‘Are they?’

‘They think so.’

‘What does that mean?

‘It means the deal you did with them was a bad deal for you but they are sticking to it. The refining process begins with extraction and all extraction has two results. When you have taken something out of ground, or the sea or the air, it’s gone. The processing involves huge amounts of helium, which is used to cool the particle accelerators under the desert and also the superconducting magnets the process uses. Remember the cold you felt in the tunnels? Helium is abundant in the universe but it’s rare here. When it’s released into the atmosphere it escapes into space and when it’s gone, it’s gone forever. In a very short time you will also run out of rare earth elements . All the technology you’ve come to rely on over the last century will fail. No more computers, phones, satellites, medical scanners. They’ll all fail irreparably and the result will be chaos, war, mass starvation and epidemics. The end of civilization for all but an elite. But that was the deal.'

'How could that be the deal? Who with?'

'Your people,' said the man in white. 'It's just business.'

'What will happen to Earth?'

'Pollution.'

'How bad?

'The craft they travel leave a plasma trail. The very first time one visited it started a chemical reaction – the atmosphere has begun polymerizing. The process is accelerating to a tipping point. The effect is leeching down from the stratosphere. Eventually, your atmosphere will solidify. It's ironic. Everything is melting. But your air will encase the planet like amber. It will be like a marble spinning in space.'

'We're all going to die?'

'If you mean your species: Not all of you. Some will go to an exoplanet.'

'And do what?'

'They didn't ask.'

'That doesn't sound good.'

'No.'

'Are they going to be colonizing this planet?'

'In a way. But not for humanity. They believe they are going in an ark but it is more in the nature of a slave ship. With a breeding program. They will survive, hence the abductions carried out by the Grays for the Tall Whites over the past half-century. But they'll wish they hadn't.'

'Can't you stop it?'

'The exodus? The deal has been struck.'

'My god. What about the rest of us? What about the air?'

'The pollution is reversible – eventually – if you catch it now.'

'So you could stop it?'

'The Tall Whites could.'

'Why don't they?'

'It isn't in the contract.'

'Can't you do something?'

'Nothing direct. The Greater Community would not permit it.'

'You can't or you won't?'

'Nothing direct.'

'Why are you telling me this now. Is it because you know I won't remember?' Mike's brain roiled. There had to be a way to beat this. There had to be.

There was a noise behind him. He turned and saw a Tall White alien crouching as she came through the door. Beside her was Colonel Baxter.

'I have to go, Mike,' said the man in white. 'I'm sorry.'

Chapter Fourteen
Generations

Boston. MA. Present

The media had no way into Creech. The whole of the Nellis ranges were off limits, ostensibly to avoid interfering with first search and recovery then the investigation. If Mike had been around he would have made some kind of joke about being the obstacles multiplying exponentially but to Doug it just added up to one huge professional challenge. The weak spot in Creech's perimeter was General Snow, the self-aggrandizing PX ranger nominally in charge of the drone base. A Pentagon contact plus a few well-directed blandishments had secured Snow's cooperation. It was legitimate in so far as Doug was making plausible efforts to raise the funding for a documentary on the Redtail crash and the mystery of Mike's whereabouts. Snow was unaware that Doug had chosen as its working title, "Missing in Dreamland", in recognition of the prevailing belief among U.F.O. watchers in the existence of aliens at the Nellis Ranges. Along with the Bermuda Triangle, Bigfoot and the Titanic, the term Area 51 (which was only part of the area they were supposed to inhabit) was enough to get producers' juices running. It didn't matter how little new information (if any) you presented or how many times you repeated the same questions without answering them, people would watch. Doug called it ritual TV. The same went for anything with Nazis, psycho killers and apparitions. The trouble was that Doug was sailing under false colors, aiming to carry out a genuine investigation instead of simply working to the formula. The air crash inquiry was going to be under wraps for a long while and the issue of homeland security lurked in the background. Out of nowhere, websites had begun running, first threads, then full-blown stories – all curiously similar – that the Feds suspected Mike of causing the crash, even though there was no sign of him on the F.B.I.'s Most Wanted list, nor, indeed any acknowledgment, anywhere that anyone official was interested in his whereabouts. Which in itself was fishy. Doug found himself descending into classic conspiracy theory territory: if absence of proof wasn't proof of absence, the absence of any acknowledged investigation was deeply sinister. But, no doubt Mike would soon appear on YouTube at the mall with Elvis so that no-one with any credibility could raise the subject of Mike and be taken seriously. Doug kept these thoughts to himself and made his pitch as rationally and as commercially as he was able, in person in L.A. and on Skype in New York. Boston was a non-starter. The ritual TV angle appealed but only if Doug could do it in a week end-to-end, preferably with crappy video to make it look authentic. 'Blair Witch Project' meets 'World's Weirdest Disaster Mysteries'. When higher-minded network executives and producers questioned Doug's ability to present the story dispassionately, Doug ran with it: his partisanship and working from the 'personal angle' would give the film more appeal. If he could find Mike, it would make fantastic viewing, especially given the allegations that were starting to surface. Trouble was, no one knew how to categorize the story; it was neither news nor history, U.F.O. revelation nor 'True Crime', and it could easily go haywire if Mike were arrested the day after it was released. That scenario appealed to the online insiders but Doug was 'the science guy', not Michael Moore. Thanks for coming by. Keep in touch. Loser.

Doug's satellite phone buzzed into life.

'Are we clear to talk?' asked Brandy.

'Sure,' said Doug. 'Give me a minute.'

Doug pulled the window shut and switched on the gizmo he had bought on the net to vibrate the pane so no-one could eavesdrop by laser. He knew the apartment was clean. Jemma had asked one of the university's security guys how to sweep it for bugs, and his mobile was sitting in his ice box. He was still pretty sure all this was unnecessary, but Jemma, by way of Bob, had been insistent.

'Hi. We can talk now,' he told Brandy. 'Apparently, we have an extra layer of encryption Jemma developed, herself, so we can say what we like. Name someone you want bump off. Someone real important.'

'Not even in jest,' said Brandy. 'Listen. This is pure gold. Bob kind of gave it away that he knows someone who actually works at Creech. He didn't name names but those drone jocks have to be in complete denial or half-psycho. One guy could have killed hundreds of people, and there has to be collateral, including children. It's a lot for a man's conscience or his sense of duty to bear.'

'Granted but how does that help us?'

'Our man – or woman – could hold it together except for one thing: some of them are right here in the U.S.A. On the air base.'

'They test weapons.'

'On live targets?'

'You're saying we have been using drones, with lethal force, here in the U.S? Jesus. On prisoners of war? Jihadists? Who? Soldiers?'

'I spoke to the sheriff at Indian Springs. I got along a lot better with Zane than you did. I asked him about missing persons and he let slip about a hunter who vanished a day before the air crash. The sheriff was out looking for him when the plane came down and the case has been on hold ever since.'

'A guy with a red pick-up?'

'How did you know?'

'Doesn't matter.'

'Bob asked his source if anything had happened the night before the crash. They have been testing something called a Coyame device, some kind of sound bomb that can be tuned to kill people based on their physical make-up.'

'For a race war?'

'Possibly. They have been working on it since the Vietnam era. I guess that would make sense. The point is that he used it that night. It didn't sink in until he was back home and it made him sick to his stomach.'

'What says he isn't just some burnt-out fruit loop?'

'Bob says he was anxious and depressed, not deranged. A whistleblower. When the hunter went missing it was all on screen. The device worked. One guy died but the others in the area… well he said they weren't human but obviously he must have got that wrong… They were unharmed.'

'Maybe it doesn't work very well. Or it's short range?'

'Sure. I don't buy this alien stuff but get this: They wanted him to deploy it again, using a drone. They had another intruder but he was way up in an area where no goes without the highest clearance, way, way above Top Secret. Only, this time, they couldn't use it. The target was protected.'

'Who by?'

'That's just it. This guy says aliens but the point is that, that is where Mike was. That guy could be Mike.'

'Brandy: you're a genius. I owe you.'

'This may not be the time, but I think I also found a clue as to what happened to your granddaddy. I found photocopies of a journal that I made when I was at Colombia. It didn't make any sense at the time but I think there could be a connection between your granddaddy's disappearance and Mike's. It's to do with the last entry. The date.'

'The date?'

'Yes. 16 October, 1972.'

'The day he vanished.'

'There's a name by the date.'

'What is it?

'H.B. Juneau? Does it mean anything to you?'

'No. I don't think so.'

'I'll scan it and send it over.'

Doug took the first available flight to Las Vegas and read his grandfather's notes on the flight. Then he got back to the business in hand: finding Bob and locating Mike. It took far longer than he hoped to track down Bob Tilson. The shiny trailer had vanished. Ray, the barkeep at the Space Station had denied all knowledge of him. When Doug pressed the point, Ray produced a broken pool cue and threatened to smash it over Doug's head. Doug took the hint. Marlene stopped Doug in the trailer park and told him Bob had cleared out after his trailer had been seized, with all its contents. Bob was a good guy, she said, a believer. She'd spent many a long night 'hopin' to see what he seen.' Ray had sold Bob his old Shovelhead Electroglide, a tarp and a handgun. 'He said he was headed to the Summit Lake reservation but that motor sickle ain't no good for cross-country,' she said. 'Reckon Bob's in Las Vegas, if he ain't just kept going.'

Doug figured she was probably right and anyway he needed a base with Wifi. When he checked his cell, he was surprised to find a cryptic text from Crazy Becca. Bob was occupying a one-room apartment near U.S. 95. It was on the second floor with a door reached by a fragile-looking wooden staircase. The apartment next door was burned out, the windows were all busted out and the walls above the shattered windows, blackened. The smell of charred wood and burnt paint still hung over it. Doug tested the stairs before climbing them and rapped at the door. When he got no answer, he pushed a business card under the door and went back to his car. As he turned onto Jones Boulevard a voice behind him said, 'Don't look round. Just keep driving – normal.' Doug looked into the driver's mirror and saw no one.

'Jesus, Bob. You trying to kill us both?'

'Just keep driving. Have you got a cell?'

'Yes'

'Give it to me.'

'What's this all about Bob?'

'Just give it to me.'

Doug handed over his phone. He could hear Bob taking out the battery and heard the snap of a metal glasses case.

Bob stayed hunkered down. 'Becca told me you

were coming. We spoke just before the Feds stole my trailer.'

'Did they set the fire where you're living now.'

'No. That was an accident. The guy next door was a junkie. If they knew where I was I'd be wearing orange by now.'

'Brandy told me about the drone. The device they've been testing,' said Doug. 'We found some old papers of my granddaddy's. And it made me wonder if you weren't right about that some of that stuff you came up with.'

'Hallelujah,' said Bob.

'Among a list of place names was Coyame. I looked it up and that was where a spacecraft was supposed to have crashed into Mexico in the Sixties. U.S. troops went over the border illegally and recovered it. There's two versions of what happened next. In both, the Mexican Army get there first. Our guys arrive and find them all dead. One theory is we killed them, which would have been an act of war. And murder. Another is that there was some kind of radiation. Either way, they hauled off the remains of the spaceship and its crew, and burned everything. I mean really burned. For whatever reason the Mexicans went along with the cover-up. My guess is that what killed those Mexican soldiers was the basis for the Coyame device.'

'Welcome to my world.'

'Do you really you think they have got him?'

'Are the Kennedys gun-shy?' said Bob. 'What else you got?'

Bob had waited until Doug put the car through a car wash at dusk, before clambering over into the front seat. They drove to a diner and found an inside seat facing the door. Doug showed Bob the journal Brandy had found.

'There wasn't a great deal of solid material in here, mainly lists. But there was a piece that made me laugh at first about Eisenhower disappearing during a golfing vacation and some prankster running a story he was dead,' said Doug.

'Palm Springs,' nodded Bob.

'Err, yes. It was,' said Doug.

'Ike did a deal with the aliens there and then came back and signed Public Law 28 into being so he could steal Indian land and give it to the extraterrestrials.'

'Indian land?' said Doug, bemused. He looked in the driver's mirror. The road behind seemed clear.

'My mother was a British war bride but my old man was a Paiute Indian up here in Nevada. He won the Air Medal over in Europe. They called native Americans 'chiefs' but when they came back they got no respect. Eisenhower didn't think our ways fit with the American Way. More than twenty five thousand Indians served in the armed services but the Government didn't think they were American enough so they brought in nearly fifty termination laws. They revoked all the old one-sided treaties and put the natural resources on Indian land up for grabs. They used the Termination Laws to buy off bands like the Agua Caliente in Palm Springs with casinos and then mine the land underneath them, except they weren't mining, they were building an underground city for aliens.'

'Casinos come into my granddaddy's journal. He must have thought there was something more than just mob business going on in Las Vegas, maybe tied in with Intelligence and perhaps even the C.I.A,' said Doug.

'Nellis, Frenchman's Flat, Groom, S-4, all that area. With nuclear tests, stealth planes, drones and the like they can keep the whole world away from there and keep the aliens happy,' said Bob. 'I told you. I've seen scout craft and alien freighters coming in and out of there. It's a big, big operation and it takes a lot of organization.'

'You still believe Mike's being held by aliens and a parallel government?'

'Look. I have seen the aliens. So has Mike. Steve found him in the desert with sunstroke even though the temperature had been down near zero and it was night. How do you explain that?'

'I can't but let's say there are aliens and say they have him.'

'They have him. They have him. O.K? They give off something that can make your body haywire. Sunstroke.'

'Alright. Let's agree there are aliens. What is this about a parallel government?'

Bob clicked the radio on. Some syndicated shock jock was bawling away about liberals. He re-tuned to a station playing Dean Martin.

'There's big money involved and its all black economy,' Bob explained. 'You can't run an operation this size for this long in secret without a huge network or without using dubious methods: murder, mind control, the drugs trade. War. War is a good one, that's really expensive and really hard to keep track of when a single Tomahawk missile officially costs more than a million and half bucks. "Oh heck. We just lost one. Too bad. And it's the bottom of the sea so there's no accounting for it. Aw shucks." If you really want to throw up a smoke screen, you wash it all through private firms. You know there were more private contractors – that's mercenaries to you and me – in Iraq than U.S. troops, and you had the secretary for defense handing single-bidder contracts to his own corporation. Man, that stinks on any level but when you add in the aliens…'

'There have always been insider trading, graft, fraud, theft, ghost budgets, fake invoices. You don't need a parallel government for that,' Doug interrupted. 'There are whole government departments, the Congressional Budget Office, the I.R.S., tens of thousands of people all paid to dig this stuff up.'

'And they're really great at what they do, aren't they? The whole of our legitimate government comes to halt every couple of years while the world turns. When Eisenhower was President the alien program was all paid for with money laundered through the mob,' said Bob. 'Now, they don't need the mob. There's at least thirty trillion dollars supposedly stashed in the private bank accounts of the super-rich. So much for trickle-down economics. Even in a world where fewer than a hundred people own more wealth than the poorest third of the entire population, that's a hell of a lot of money to be sitting around unused and unaccounted for. Of course it's being used, it's a parallel economy and it's run by a secret elite that been operating off the books with aliens for nearly seventy years. And that is who has your friend Mike.'

'Why haven't they killed him?'

'That is a bigger mystery, my man.'

'Where do you think he is?'

'My bet is Creech.'

'Why are we going down town?'

'To meet the others. Take a right.'

Doug was surprised to find Jemma, Steve and, above all, Crazy Becca, waiting at the Tropicana, Las Vegas. They were waiting in an all-white suite with doors out to the pool area. The doors were shut and the drapes pulled against the urban glow.

'We spoke on the 'Undernet', the part of the web the feds can't listen in on,' said Bob.

'Coffee?' volunteered Becca from the kitchenette. 'Fair Trade, decaf, with almond milk. You will like it.'

'Almond?' said Steve. 'You know how much cesium and strontium there is in almonds?'

'Don't get cranky Steve,' laughed Doug. 'I am delighted to see you but what the heck are you guys all doing here?'

'These guys think they got a lead on Mike,' said Steve, indicating Bob and Becca.

'Bob and I got talking as soon as the plane crashed,' said Becca.

'Why didn't you tell me you were meeting up?'

'We had to move quick,' said Jemma. 'I had been trying to hack in to Creech…'

'Are you insane? Haven't you ever heard of Edward Snowden or Gary McKinnon?' spluttered Doug. 'We could all end up shot against a wall.'

'You gotta listen, Doug,' said Becca. 'Both those guys have come up with evidence of an alien conspiracy.'

'It seems to be true,' said Jemma. 'McKinnon found a list of non-terrestrial officers when he was poking around the NASA systems and posting "Your security is crap" on military sites. He got in through the support and logistics. Once you're in, you're O.K, because they all think you're one of them. All you have to do then is to move from one trusting network to another using network status. The list was of officers on ships – craft – that weren't listed as naval vessels. The LeMay and the Hillenkoetter, both named after senior military figures associated with U.F.O.s'

'Majestic,' said Bob. 'They were both in Majestic. It's a secret committee of top scientists, military personnel and business people who are working with the aliens. Look at this picture. It's John F. Kennedy swearing in Curtis LeMay as Air Force chief. Look. Right here. '

'I still don't buy it,' said Steve.

'Those craft are secret spacecraft and they're being prepared to take an elite to a handful of exoplanets to start colonies when Earth is all used up, and that's the truth,' said Becca.

'You're basing this on the word of a hacker who is a self-confessed, autistic toker,' sighed Steve. 'Some delusional prankster who only escaped a seventy year sentence because the British wouldn't extradite him.'

'But Snowden had evidence too,' said Becca. 'There's hundreds of files on these Tall White aliens and technology transfers, and huge ark-like space ships out there. He even has evidence that we already had a colony on the moon in the Sixties.'

'Does he? Hell!' said Steve. 'Doug. Tell them where that story came from.'

'Whether you think Snowden was a traitor or not he blew the whistle on the U.S. and the U.K. governments' spying operations against all of us. Mass, illegal sweeps of every kind of digital communications. That much is fine by me. It had to be exposed but what Bob and you are talking about is a story that some lazy asshole at an Iranian agency lifted wholesale from a fringe website. It was penned by a lone religious nut with no connection to Snowden. It's fiction and it's a blind.'

'That's what they want you to think,' said Bob. 'Wheels within wheels.'

'These are the same people who claim the Tall Whites were helping the Nazis build atomic submarines in World War Two.'

'They could have been,' said Becca indignantly.

'Can I remind you who won the war?' asked Doug.

Steve's patience was wearing thin. 'And why would they go through the entire Apollo program if they already had a base on the moon?'

'I don't know. Maybe, because there was a base on the moon, you know? Because if they didn't go through that charade they would have to say how they really got there.' Becca was warming up, now.

'They are institutionally incapable of telling the truth,' Bob said. 'They have cleared up a dozen U.F.O crash sites since Roswell in 1947 and they have lied about all of them. They lied about Kennedy. They lied about the moon landings. They lied about the Twin Towers…'

'Now wait a second,' said Steve. 'The Twin Towers? You're saying the U.S. Government hijacked planes and killed hundreds of American citizens? To what end?'

'…No. They didn't kill them directly. But they let it happen. Because they wanted a war to cover up the cost of their deal with the aliens.'

'If you're looking for a conspiracy, look at the cover-up of the illnesses and deaths that came out of the demolition and construction work,' Steve snarled, 'but don't dishonor the people who died on 9/11 by claiming they weren't murdered by terrorists. You never heard of the 9/11 Commission?'

'An inside job,' said Bob. 'Like Kennedy and the Warren Commission. Warren couldn't even count to four. Four shots that's how many in the Zapruder film. But Warren says there was only three. So there was only three. But everyone knows there was another shot from another direction. And there two types of bullet. If he fired anything at all, Oswald fired metal-jacketed bullets. The bullet that blew Kennedy's brains out was a soft nose. It's in the medical records.'

'The House Select Committee on Assassinations did actually say that,' Doug agreed. 'They did say there were four shots. They were really pretty down on the F.B.I.'s investigation. That ought to prove something even if it's that things get put right in the end.'

'Yes and what they said was refuted by the National Academy of Sciences,' said Steve. Having vented, he added, 'although, for the record, the medical evidence sucks…'

'It's the old switcheroo' said Bob. 'Oh my God.' He pointed at the last entry of Douglas Reeder's journal. 'Oh my God.'

'What?' Doug demanded.

'H.B. Juneau, October 12, 1972. H.B. That's Hale Boggs. He was a congressman on the Warren Commission but he didn't go along with it. We've always said he was about to blow the lid on the Kennedy assassination when he went missing. So, it's true.'

'Yes. Yes. I remember, now. On a plane up in Alaska,' said Doug. 'A Cessna, with a military pilot. And there was another congressman. There was a huge search that went on for weeks but it came up with nothing. I researched it. Small planes have had to carry emergency locater devices ever since.'

'And you know who drove Boggs to the airport? A young Bill Clinton, that's who,' chirped Becca.

'So what?' said Steve.

'Just saying,' said Becca.

Bob pointed at the journal entry again. 'This says to me Douglas Reeder boarded that plane at Juneau to interview Boggs and went down with it. Boggs was going give him the full story behind Kennedy and the alien conspiracy,' Bob declared. 'That's what we're up against, man.'

'One last, big story. A nuclear bomb of a story that blow everything away. He'd have had to have had solid corroboration.'

Jemma had stayed quiet. 'There is more,' she said. 'I found more.' Steve and Doug caught each other's eye. Each saw a look that said 'something wicked this way comes.'

'Don't tell you me you actually broke into a military network?' said Doug, slowly, word by word.

'I couldn't get into Creech. They sealed it off hermetically since the drone control systems were hacked with a keystroke reader in 2011,' said Jemma, 'and unlike civil aviation, the 24th Air Force, has never joined up all the armed forces networks. It's safer that way but it is also just the way they developed. Nothing is standardized.' Doug looked relieved. 'Which is why I was able to hack an old Fortran-based system at NORAD…'

'Jesus Christ!' Doug spluttered. 'NORAD? The North American Aerospace Defense Command? Nuclear Central?'

'Yes. I got in through its Santa tracking system. They get letters to Santa and they put them on file!' said Jemma. 'They have been doing it for decades.'

'You couldn't make it up,' said Bob.

'By hopping networks I got to the Air Force O.S.I., and they have or at least had a survivor from the RedTail crash,' said Jemma, 'at a facility inside Creech at Dog Bone Lake. It must be Mike.'

'That's where the Tall Whites are,' cried Bob, triumphantly.

'So all we have to do it to find a way to break into a top secret military establishment, find him and snatch him away from under the multiple noses of some bug-eyed monster with a ray gun,' said Steve. 'Genius! What are we waiting for?'

'Don't rush on our account,' said a voice from behind.

Jemma recognized the Air Force cop and the man with him, the silent one who had 'called' on her. Bob knew him too: from the picture of Kennedy and Curtis LeMay, standing a row back from the ceremony, watching from behind dark glasses. The same bullet-headed guy only now, fifty years later, he wore white. They were followed by a woman in military uniform. Jemma caught sight of blue lights flashing on the pool. They were surrounded. The five friends were led out to black, plain-sided vans and put into them separately, each with an armed guard and a driver. They each sat in a rear-facing seat, opposite their captors. Traveling backwards made it harder to judge how far or fast they travelled but the journey seemed to take about twenty minutes, with no stops, which must have meant no red lights or intersections.

When the van halted the door slid open and Doug could see the others being led towards a passenger jet. With a shudder, Doug recognized it as a Boeing 737, the same type of plane that had crashed with Mike and Gary in it. It was white with a red cheat line along its side. His heart sank. It was a U.R.S. plane, from 'Janet', the civilian airline used by the Air Force and the C.I.A. And that, he surmised, was the Janet terminal at McCarran. Everyone on board, including all the flight attendants would have top security clearance. His heart sank further as he figured they were either being taken to Langley or Guantanamo Bay. Neither prospect filled him with joy.

Doug, Jemma and the others were shown to window seats whose blinds were drawn. A fed sat next to each of them. No one talked.

It was a long flight. It was hard to judge time – as if they had been in a casino – but he had a feeling they must have crossed the entire country. When the military woman signaled to the agents to move up front, Steve took his opportunity and raised the blind. Day had broken. They were over an urban area but flying real low. Way too low for a regular passenger jet. Maybe two thousand feet, the height they had jumped from. They must be busting all the rules. Why would they want to attract attention like that?

The military woman stood in the aisle and addressed them.

'My name is Major Shirley Kirby, U.S.A.F. You are all here because you think you know something about what happens on the facility at Creech Air Force Base and you believe that that has a connection to RedTail Flight 488. You believe that the U.S. Air Force has been holding Michael Roland captive since the strike on Creech and that this has been at the behest of a secretive group that has mounted a conspiracy with a number of extraterrestrial alien species. You have been involved in a serious breach of national security in a time of high-level threat to the U.S. homeland and U.S. citizens and forces around the world.

'Shit,' muttered Bob. 'This is it. I should have known you were too good to be true.'

'It is the seriousness of that threat that has forced us to take radical action,' said Kirby. 'You are about to meet Michael Roland for the first time since the strike…'

Jemma's heart leapt into her throat. Ice ran down her spine. Had she heard right? Mike was here on this plane?

'… but you must understand that he has been through a great deal and he may not be as you would expect, or hope.'

'Oh my God, thought, Jemma. 'What has happened to you Mike?'

Mike stood before them supported gently under one elbow by the man. He looked thin and pale. He had lank hair and the start of a beard. There he stood, like an escapee from a dungeon, peering at them with intelligence but no recognition.

'Mike,' shouted Jemma as she rose and moved as fast as she could towards him. He saw her approaching fast but looked to one side to see who she was addressing.

'Mike. You're alive and… oh my god, are you O.K.?' said Jemma, her words falling out like spilled beads.

'I'm fine,' said Mike, looking first at Jemma and then the others. 'I don't know where we are.'

'Nor do we Mike. Oh, Mike, are you O.K?' Tears slipped down Jemma's cheeks.

Mike looked at each of them for a clue.

Steve gently moved Jemma away and sat Mike down. 'It's Steve, Mike. I'm Steve.' He could see Mike struggling to mesh the name and the face. 'I am a doctor, Mike. I am going to check you out.' He held a finger upwards and asked Mike to follow it with his eyes. The he listened to Mike's chest and felt his pulse.' Any pain, apart from your head and your arm?' Mike shook his head. 'Do you know what day it is? 'Mike shook his head again. 'What's your other name, Mike?'

'Mike?' he ventured.

Steve looked round to Jemma. 'Looks like damage to the medial temporal lobe or the hippocampus, probably occasioned by the crash. Retrograde and anterograde amnesia. Signs of hemiparesis, judging by that arm, and possible dyspraxia. He'll need a scan.'

Mike looked round at them, one by one. Steve noted that he was oddly etiolated and scrawny but otherwise in good condition. His movements appeared normal other than the arm that seemed to hang so heavily. But he was vacant. Not empty-headed. He had lost none of his native intelligence. His mind was a blank.

'Mike,' said Jemma, 'Please try to remember me. I love you, baby.'

And she saw a light slowly ignite in Mike's eyes.

'Jemma?' he asked. 'Jemma?'

'New York? Are you kidding me? There's been

another air crash. All flights in and out of Las Vegas have been grounded or diverted. I gotta cover it.' Doug could hear Brandy's determination.

'Trust me. This is bigger.'

'Bigger? How can it be bigger?'

'Do you want an exclusive on the biggest story in history?'

There was silence for two beats. Then: 'I must be nuts.'

'You'll thank me.'

"I'll do something to you.'

The K.L.V.H. van pulled up outside Brandy's condo. Ray, the camera operator, was game for anything. Never asked why or how, only where, when and what? She calculated that they could reach New York in under thirty-six hours, collecting violations, taking shifts at the wheel and only stopping for fuel and the washroom. Violations she could do without. The washroom, she could improvise. There was a lot of roadside between Las Vegas and New York.

The highways out of Vegas were unusually busy and all the traffic was heading out of town. 'Kind of spooky. Like animals sensing an earthquake,' said Ray.

Doug interviewed Mike, who relayed everything he could recall of his experience at Creech, plus all the details that the man in white had given him, the history of Majestic and the alien conspiracy, the secrecy, the lies, and the terrible, terrible future that lay ahead unless the deals done by Ike and the others were broken.

Mike had done what the man in white asked. With an almost superhuman effort he had mapped practically every moment of his life. He had assigned a number and a set to all the important incidents and some that appeared trivial, all the highs and lows, the tastes, the sounds, the totems, the passion, every aspect of his life with Jemma, even the regrets and failures, building them into a huge math landscape, a journey he made repeatedly as a mnemonic, and he had made the light that guided him that phrase in Jemma's mouth: 'I love you, baby.' If he could not hear those words, he did not want to remember. She was his life and without her he did not want it back. But she had said it. 'I love you, baby.' And if his feat of memorizing had been like some defragging process with every part of his brain lighting up for Christmas, files were erased, but those that were left were sharper and contiguous. His past was a three dimensional map with every pathway illuminated and signed; his present offered no reference other than the people around him; all their futures were uncharted.

'What about you?' Doug said to the man in white. 'Are you going on the record?' It was the first time Mike had seen him laugh. He shook his head.

'No but I will consider your questions.'

'You say you are a kind of umpire, a regulator. And that you can't intervene in our affairs. And yet you have.'

'I am here to see that the rules are adhered to. You made a deal, a series of deals. And you delivered your side of the bargain. The Tall Whites stick to the letter of an agreement but not always its spirit. You did not give them a deadline for the technology transfer they promised or specify it had to be delivered here on Earth. You expected mental control, faster-than-light travel; you got Teflon.'

'Faster than light travel!' Steve interjected. 'See, that's where I have a problem with all this. Faster than light travel just isn't possible.'

'It might be if you rethought the geometry of space time,' said Mike. He took a strip of paper and turned one end, holding them together with his finger and thumb. 'If I trace a continuous line along one side you'll see that it goes along the "inside" and the "outside". Our eyes tell us it's a three dimension object but it only has one side.'

'A Mobius strip,' said Steve. 'O.K….'

'Yes. And there are variations on this like the Klein bottle. If you take two Mobius strips with opposite orientations and put them together you get what is called a Klein bottle. You take this further to Boy's Surface and on. They are complex, multidimensional but still have just one surface.'

'You're losing me.'

'Let's say space time is homeomorphic. It's stretched and pulled, maybe by singularities, black holes. If space time is knitted together from an infinite number of single dimension topologies you could travel distances that would be impossible measured along the length of each volume's "surface", simply by moving across them and slipping from one to the next and the next and so on. That's what you meant by the dark matter matrix, isn't it?'

The man in white shrugged. 'Could be.'

'They can travel thirty times the speed of light,' Bob declared. 'It would only take them a month to get to Alpha Centauri, except they're not welcome there anymore.'

'Or there's Alcubierre,' Mike continued. He was on a roll. It made Jemma's heart melt. He was back. 'Miguel Alcubierre reckoned you could use negative mass to warp space time and overcome time dilation. The key is exotic matter. I'm also guessing there's less actual dark matter than we think, though. Maybe it just doesn't interact with light.' He unfurled the Mobius strip and frantically began drawing a chart linking boxes containing the names Minkowski, Cuachy and de Sitter, each branching into a set of equations.

'If I remember right,' said Doug, 'the speed of light depends on the medium. It's about three quarters as fast in water as it is in space, so particles, cosmic rays or whatever, that are still flying around at full speed could travel faster than light in, say, a pool.'

'But the speed of light in a vacuum is still the ultimate limit,' insisted Steve, appealing to the man in white, who simply said: 'Not my field.'

'So that's how you're making good on the deal?' said Doug. 'You've given Mike the tools to make the technology leap himself.'

'Not just Mike. He's important, but so are all of you. You have to work together.'

'But why now?'

'There is going to be a take-over,' said the man in white.

'I thought they had already taken over.'

'The non-humans you did a deal with are being bought out. They'll re-organize. Divide the world into four areas of operation. Take resources from a wider area. Likely use pink noise to subdue you. A deal is already being brokered with China.'

'You know it always seemed weird to me that the aliens only dealt with the good old U.S. of A. How come?' asked Steve.

'It does make sense,' said Doug. 'It really does. We were the only superpower back then. Sixty years earlier it would have been the British. Now it's the Chinese. The People's Liberation Army have been running banks, mines, the Chinese space program, for decades. It's the military-industrial complex writ large. The whole upper echelon of the Party could be Majestic for all anyone knows, and probably is.' He paused. 'So, we're being sold up the river?'

'The Tall Whites will no longer be obliged to complete their bargain with you. The aliens that will be in charge are asset strippers. The Tall Whites might still be persuaded to remediate and repair the damage done by plasma trails but the new race will not think it worth the investment.'

'Plasma trails?' asked Steve.

Mike's diagram was now a tortuous web covering various scraps of paper laid out on the table. 'There are four states of matter,' he said, distractedly. 'Gas, liquid, solid and plasma. You can create plasma with microwaves or atomic fusion or magnetism. It's the most abundant form of matter in the universe so it makes sense they'd use it in some form. What seems to happen is that when these alien craft enter our atmosphere at the Karman Line they trail filaments of plasma that are suspended in the air, kind of like the droplets of cream in a coffee. Eventually they build up and the ordinary matter around them begins to behave differently. At first, some falls to Earth as particulates and the rest just hangs there like house dust. Because the molecules at the interface between the plasma and the other matter are charged, the filaments are held where they are by repulsion but eventually they lose their charge and begin to join up in long chains, polymers, potentially billions or trillions of molecules long. The air turns to plastic.'

'Plastic planet. We'd go back to where it was pretty much before life evolved,' said Steve. 'No photosynthesis. Maybe a few tube worms deep in the ocean at vents in the sea floor. They'd be the dominant species. Or maybe some anaerobic bacteria. Jesus.'

'This is what alien craft leave behind them in our atmosphere, right?' asked Doug. 'So it's like the ozone layer and C.F.Cs, when the chemical shit in refrigerators and aerosols went up into the sky and ripped open a hole in the ozone layer and started to let in ultraviolet? Donny, the medical air investigator, said he'd heard something about catastrophic engine failure in relation to the Redtail crash. An atmospheric anomaly. Are we talking about the same thing?'

The man in white slowly nodded again.

Bob's eyes widened. 'So it was brought down by an alien scout craft. But not by a hit: by the crap from its exhaust. Wow.'

Doug asked, 'how do we know where they are? They used satellites to spot the hole in the ozone layer. Maybe they could find these plasma trails the same way.'

'The International Space Station,' said Bob.

'Huh?'

'There's a ton of video showing craft entering the atmosphere. They claim it's space junk. I kind of ignored it but the other thing, which I just thought was, like, "interesting but so what?", because I assumed it was natural, was they keep seeing the Northern Lights where they shouldn't be.'

'The aurora?' asked Doug.

'Yeah. But not like drapes, more like balls of light.'

'Cherenkov radiation,' said Mike. 'Caused by

charged particles around the plasma traveling faster than the light itself as it entered the atmosphere.'

'Thing is,' said Bob. 'They've started appearing all over the globe. Over deserts. Peru, Namibia, the Gobi desert, the Sinai, not just Arizona.'

'They're landing on every continent,' said Doug. 'Which means the aliens are going everywhere and there's no part of the atmosphere that won't be affected.'

'They must be doing deals with everyone,' said Bob. 'The Russians. The ayatollahs. You name it'

'Why bother with governments when corporations have bigger budgets and no-one to rein them in?' said Doug.

'You know?' said Steve. 'Maybe you're right and maybe we deserve it.'

'They had to model chlorofluorocarbons,' said Jemma. 'You would have to know how the plasma behaves in order to deal with it. Could you model it?'

'In principle,' said Mike. 'You would have to be able to differentiate to orders of Lucas numbers. I can't see how that's possible. Please tell me I'm wrong, but we just don't have that kind of computer power. Do we?'

'We could have, if we were to use a grid,' said Jemma. 'If we were to link up every PC and supercomputer on the net, I could write an app that would enable you to harness every spare bit of computing power on Earth. You would just have to give me the formula.'

'Well that's us screwed,' said Steve. 'If one tenth of what you have said is true, there's no way these Majestics would let us link up everyone on the whole internet if it was going to expose them.'

'Unless they were exposed another way,' said Doug.

'What the…?'

'Huh?' Brandy's attention had drifted. But the van was still dead center of the highway; nothing coming the other way, only a few lights, way back. Ahead: a false dawn and the New Jersey Turnpike.

'Sorry,' she said.

'Not you. This,' said Ray. He held the phone. The screen dazzled Brandy.

'What is this?'

'Another plane.'

'We knew that.'

'No. I mean one more has crashed near Las Vegas. They're calling it the Nevada Triangle.'

'Gimme. Gimme.' Ray handed her the phone. 'Take the wheel,' she said, and read. 'This thing keeps updating. They're falling out of the sky like a plague of Egypt.'

'You sure we're still headed the right way?' asked Ray.

'My head says no. My gut says yes.'

'Good enough for me.'

Doug had everything ready for the next stage. Revelation was essential. Majestic and the whole network of deception and exploitation flourished in the half-light of secrecy. It needed a worldwide audience and credibility, after decades of disinformation. Douglas Reeder had been on the right trail. Doug would finish his grandfather's work. He owed it to him even though he knew that most sane people who saw the interview would dismiss it as another sad hoax, cult-fodder – well produced, but cult-fodder for all that. Those that did believe it would ignore it just like they ignored climate change, the poverty a block away, their own lack of liberties. The corruption. They needed incontrovertible proof that Mike was telling the truth and that something had to be done to expose the reality of a conspiracy against humanity – a human conspiracy against the human race; by no means the first but likely the final conspiracy.

Baxter knew that too, and he was on his way.

'If thou hast no sympathy for the troubles of others, thou art unworthy to be called by the name of a human.'

'What's that?' asked Doug.

'That is from a Persian poem. And it's on a wall in there,' said Brandy, indicating the U.N. Building, 'but I guess we'll have to make do with stock footage unless you know someone in Safety and Security. So is this it? I hope not.'

'No. There's going to be a lot more. Look over there.'

Police, behind barriers or mounted on horseback, eyed the dense crowd of environmental protestors, a collection of predictably clownish trustafarians drumming and chanting amid more sober academics and activists, all pitting the heat of their convictions against the bitter cold of a Big Apple spring. Among them were Bob and Becca, waiting. Inside the building, one hundred fifteen world leaders, plus teams of advisers, experts, advocates, lobbyists, campaigners, speakers, secretaries and media people awaited the final address of the U.N. General Secretary. Doug pointed. Mike was visible in the passenger seat of a car bearing X plates. He was with the bullet-headed man. He and Mike strode to the delegates' entrance at First and 45th and through a cordon of sky-blue uniforms.

'We can't just walk in here, can we?' asked Mike as they made their way to the Pass and Identification Unit.

'Ambassador. Welcome back,' said an official. 'Your gold pass is ready.'

'Thank you, Ramon,' replied the man in white. 'I believe you already have received a Form S.G.6 for Mister Roland?'

'Sure thing. Here is your red pass, sir.'

As they passed through the metal detector and walked across the hall, the man in white acknowledged greetings from people who had never seen him before but knew him anyway. To Mike, he was the interstellar cop, the regulator, the man in white. To others, he was the tall, black leader of the delegation from Wherever, or the woman from Iceland, or the prince from the micro-state in the Himalayas.

'Good to see you again, sir,' said a member of staff.

'Good to be back. They have a done a good job, don't you think?' he said, waving a hand at the renovations. 'All that nicotine, finally gone forever.' The U.N. guy laughed.

The members of all six U.N. committees and representatives of the U.N. Police were gathered for a special meeting in the Security Council Chamber. The Secretary General's seat at the top of the near circular table was empty, as were those on its immediate left and right, their backs to the mural of a phoenix rising from the ashes of war. Beneath their feet, the floor, fortified with steel and concrete to protect it from bomb blasts, hung, cantilevered, over the cold, open air of F.D.R. Drive. Alternately a cocoon and a pressure cooker, that room had seen decisions made and stalled in ways that decided the lives of millions since the last official World War. There have been many wars by proxy since and mankind had continued to mine old cruelties and innovate depravity, unaware that its future was being decided elsewhere, in the shadows.

The delegates saw the Secretary General arrive accompanied by one man they all felt they knew and another who was unfamiliar. They took their places and the room grew still just as the S.G. spoke. 'Thank you all for attending this unscheduled, special meeting,' he began. 'The United Nations has faced many crises, natural and human-made but today you will hear about an urgent and desperate situation that transcends all national interests, all of issues of race, religion and geography, all concerns about natural resources, our economies, poverty, wealth, health, starvation, slavery, disease or disputes. Nothing we have faced presents us with the danger that we must first comprehend today and then find a way to overcome…'

'Oh crap, it's the guy from the base: Baxter,' gasped Mike. 'Isn't this international territory? How did he get in here?'

'That guy he's with is Air Force O.S.I. They're affiliated to Interpol.'

Baxter had convinced Close Protection of a plot against the S.G. No need for a weapon. They would do the killing for him. He saw the man in white and fleetingly recognized him. He was with the escaped prisoner. But then the ground swayed beneath his feet. He looked up to see a room full of doppelgangers. His own image. Not a reflection but each as he would see himself on film, played by dozens of actors all identical.

Dozens, no… hundreds of himself and no-one else. Not another soul. He could feel reality slipping away but forced himself to concentrate, gripping on to awareness of the illusion. No orders. No plan for this. No choice. If even a handful of humans are to survive, the Majestic plan was the only option. Majestic. Majestic. 'Don't gas-light me, you mother,' he groaned. Training kicked in. He lowered his centre of gravity and spread his weight. As he hunkered, battling with the hallucination, Baxter heard the Secretary General pronounce: 'I am here today to inform you that for decades, a small, corrupt network of individuals has been collaborating in secret with alien species, enriching themselves and risking the future of their fellow humans. Some did this knowingly, others unwittingly, so that now the human race faces disaster as great as if an asteroid were about to explode on the surface of our fragile planet and wipe the Earth clean of life. We face an extinction event and we do so because of greed and secrecy.'

The man in white spoke. In every language his message was the same: 'Aliens are among you. The Human race is no more than an expendable, exploitable resource to them. You must reclaim your planet…'

'Goddam, it,' snarled Baxter as he wrenched a side arm from a Sikh close protection officer and ran at the rostrum, squeezing the trigger.

'…and your humanity.'

The delegates dropped for cover. The guards remained transfixed. Baxter fired again and again. Mike pulled the Secretary General to the floor. The shooting stopped. For a second, there was complete silence. And then they all saw the man in white transform. Mike, Baxter, every man and woman in the room froze in awe. He was iridescent, glowing, his once human form barely discernible at the core of a field of light. Baxter looked down at his hand. The gun had gone. Had it ever been there? The crowd was draining from the room. He caught the eye of one delegate. He expected disgust or hatred or fear. He saw a strange exaltation.

EPILOG

A year later and there's no satisfactory explanation for the Nevada Triangle, although flights remain banned over Nevada and New Mexico. The drone war is still run out of Nellis. Vegas is pretty much the same but there's a new highway, built by the Army to ferry in vacationers and gamblers. The international trade treaty is going through with Asia and Europe and we're on our way to global free trade under the New World Currency Commission. Of course, there are the crazies who say we're under alien domination. They peddle scary stories of an army of extraterrestrial lizards hiding under the desert. They wail like Old Testament prophets. The end of the world is nigh. We've killed half the wildlife. We're going to war over water. We've got these atmospheric anomalies. Yada yada. We've been through this millenarian bullshit before. Time to pass round the Flavor Aid and cyanide? I don't think so. We'll find a way. We always have. As to aliens? Like the man said, 'you've got to expect some craziness.' If all that stuff about aliens conspiracy and the Government and business were true, we'd all know by now. You can't keep a secret that big for that long. Can you? And this guy, Mike Roland? The guy's clearly a whacko or worse. He's linked to the first Nevada Triangle crash and he was involved with that incident at the U.N. when some guy set fire to himself. He's not even a real American.

You ask me, the guy's nothing but a cyber terrorist. And you know what? You're probably helping him. All you suckers Roland's got working for him on his stupid 'Plasma Project' computer grid thing. You think you're cooperating, doing some good, all you 'citizen scientists' with your little computers whirring away over night, all your encrypted messages buzzing round the Undernet? You're collaborating with the enemy. That's how they rule the world, baby. Persuasion and race and gender, and all in a state of agitation, in some cases, of exhilaration but mostly plain old panic.

Aside from United Nations staff and security officials, they were experts drawn from every sphere and every institution that could reach this location without using air travel. They were called here in a completely unprecedented move, within hours of events the world has yet to comprehend. Even to take in. They were here to find out why eight planes, civilian passenger jets, military and cargo aircraft crashed in a single day in a single area being called the Nevada Triangle.

As the death toll rises, debris is scattered over thousands of square miles of the western United States. A state of emergency declared throughout the West, Nevada and New Mexico; all flights over the continental U.S.A. grounded; the worst aviation disaster in history. Its cause: still a mystery

These men and women were – are – here to find out why it happened and how to prevent a second such catastrophe, and when, if ever, it will be safe to fly again. Short of stopping a war or an epidemic, it is perhaps the most serious challenge imaginable. It is mirrored by the efforts of tens of thousands of men and women from the services, government agencies, from Park Rangers to fire fighters, the National Guard and volunteers grimly searching the crash sites for clues.

But, oddly, that was not the cause of this morning's panic at the United Nations. No. It was the appearance of an alien. A man from outer space. That's right. E.T. Mister Spock. An extraterrestrial.

Perhaps it is a measure of the febrile atmosphere within this building that so many rational and dedicated, intelligent individuals could be spooked into a stampede.

At 10.08 precisely, in that building, a man, yet to be identified, joined the General Secretary of the United Nations on the rostrum. So far, so ordinary. What happened next defies explanation.

According to witness after witness the man addressed the assembled experts – apparently in their own languages and without the need for the army of simultaneous translators who normally assist these meetings.

And (I quote directly from Professor Mary Craig-Pedersen, the Chief Scientist of the United Nations Environment Program), 'he told us we face an extinction event. The end of humanity. Of life on Earth. He told us it is being brought about by aliens and our own people. He said he was an alien. An actual alien. And then he combusted. He vanished in a bright light, like an angel, and we ran.'

Alien, angel or illusion, what is most extraordinary about this account is that it is repeated by almost everyone who was there. They are engineers, climate scientists, aviation experts. Even reporters. They all say the same. A man, to all appearances like the rest of us, spoke in tongues. He declared himself to be from the other side of the Universe. He delivered an apocalyptic warning. And then transformed into a beam of incorporeal light.

New York City Police Commissioner Alvin Chappi blames a mass hallucination. As he puts it: 'We are all scared, at this time. You have got to expect some craziness.'

The Department of Homeland Security has categorically denied that anything happened at all.

So far, there is no clue to the identity, motivation or fate of the so-called alien. Nor any hard proof of his existence. U.N. security guards have refused to release video of what happened.

The alleged event sparked a Twitterstorm among U.F.O. conspiracy theorists who link the catastrophic cluster of airplane crashes to the existence of a race of space aliens they call the Tall Whites. As evidence, they point out that the mysterious and tragic crashes occurred within an 800 mile radius of Las Vegas, which as some listeners will know, is close to Area 51, a notorious flying saucer 'hot spot' since shortly after World War Two.

Conspiracy theorists are renowned for making connections where none exist, of seeing patterns where there are none. This conspiracy theory goes further than most. It says aliens have been running a parallel government in the U.S.A. for more than half a century – after President Dwight D. Eisenhower struck a deal with creatures from outer space, for advanced technology.

Quite what Ike gave for it or got from it, they don't say. But the self-styled 'ufologists' claim it was the worst deal since the one struck in 1609 by Seyseys, the Native American chief who sold Manhattan – the island on which the United Nations building stands today – to the Dutchman Peter Minuit, for just sixty guilders, or about twenty-four dollars.

If the U.N. alien is a hoax – and I would bet my last sixty Guilders that it is – it is a cruel one and a distraction at a time of tragedy and danger. In the cosmically, mind-bogglingly, unlikely event that an alien being has delivered such a warning, and that it is true, the calamity that struck in the Nevada Triangle could be just the start, with worse, possibly far worse, to come.

My sixty guilders says that is not the case. But the fact is, the world changed this week and we can take nothing for granted, other than, as Police Commissioner Chappi put it, 'we are all scared, at this time. You have got to expect some craziness.'

This is Nick Hare, B.B.C. New York.

Endnote

If someone had come to me twenty years ago and told me stories of a Tall White alien race collaborating with the US government in a joint venture, I'd have dismissed it on the spot. Yet, here I am more than two decades later, with enough personal experience and evidence before me, to write a book on the subject – no one is more surprised about that than me.

This book is a fictional story, based on what I believe to be truth – a truth with so much compelling evidence already in the public domain, which it's hard to ignore. All I ask, dear reader, is that you approach the story with an open mind. It is the human condition to condemn ideas or belief systems that challenge our own; I simply ask that you read it and perhaps conduct a little research, before you draw your conclusions.

Let me take you back to when I first heard of the so-called 'Tall White' alien race. It was the summer of 1999, when I first met a distinguished older gentleman whom I will refer to here as John to protect his privacy – even though he is no longer with us. After World War II, John was in the UK Military in the SBS Division (known today as the Special Boat Service) and during his time in the service he became very close friends with a US army captain who was based in the UK.

Approximately one year later, the US Army Captain returned home to his wife and kids in Colorado. He kept in touch with John and many years after they first met,

John was in Colorado on business and they arranged to meet once again. John told me that the Captain had aged beyond his years and appeared to be a very disturbed man. He discovered that Captain had spent about ten years in the military, before being recruited into the Central Intelligence Service (the CIA).

After nine years with the CIA, the Captain had been assigned to a top secret operation with twenty men working under him on a classified project - one that would come to alter the course of his life. The assignment was to look after an alien life form known as the 'Tall Whites'; a race who, according to the Captain, have been interacting with humans in the military since they first made contact in the 1950s. The Captain told John that he spent six months being thoroughly briefed on the project, where he learned the extensive details of the 'joint venture' that the US Government and the Tall Whites had embarked upon.

The Captain stated that an agreement had been struck, where the Tall Whites (whom he had described as a 'far superior' race to humans) would exchange their advanced technological knowledge in exchange resources from our Earth – more on this later. It was agreed that the Tall Whites were to be given the highest grade of protection and granted exclusive rights to use the highly secure and secretive Areas 53 and 54 in the state of Nevada. Trillions of dollars had also been spent on developing a vast underground facility to further accommodate the venture.

The Captain explained that he and his team were

not allowed to approach the Tall Whites; their brief was simply to protect them from any outside human influence. He had, however, seen them on many occasions. He described them as having an incredibly pale appearance almost white in colour and very thin and tall. Their cheekbones were chiselled and their eyes larger in size than a human's. Instead of teeth they had a small curved bone like a cow's gum but thinner and had no thumbs just four fingers. Their necks were very fragile and much thinner than humans.

Now, I knew John to be a rational, worldly man and even though I took his story with a healthy dose of scepticism, it certainly unnerved me. Many years later, I came across a man called Charles Hall (whose story I suggest readers look into), who had publicly spoken out about his own experience of the alien race. His account really moved me; he explained that he had encountered the Tall Whites during his early years as a weather observer whilst in the American Air Force on Areas 53/4 in the 1960s. The similarities between John's story and Charles Hall's story were mind-blowing – Charles Hall had gone a step further than John though, explaining that the resources being taken from Earth were being sent to 'off-world' stations and an in depth understanding into their psychology .

Bringing us forward to the present day, in December 2013 a young British man named Gary Mckinnon was publicly vilified for hacking into the Pentagon's IT system, where he viewed highly sensitive, classified information. Gary gave a public interview, explaining how he had discovered a 'Non Terrestrial Officers' list and documentation regarding transfers to two off world stations. I immediately linked this to Charles Hall's account.

I recalled Charles Hall explaining how in 1967, whilst on guard at his barracks at Indiana Springs Auxiliary, he overheard the Tall Whites explaining that there are several planets outside our own solar system on which a space station could be built. He overheard talk of an agreement in which the Tall Whites would supply 'ship-to-ship transfers and take care of logistics', so long as the US Government supplied all of the hardware and labour force to build the stations. He also heard the Tall Whites request that a small docking station be built for them, in case they ever needed to pass through. For me, the light bulb moment came when it became clear that Gary Mckinnon had found information on these off-world stations on the Pentagon computer – everything was beginning to tie together.

Next I shall move forward to the curious case of infamous US 'whistle blower' Edward Snowden, who had previously worked at the Hawaii NSA underground facility. He came to learn about the giant surveillance machine that was being completed, which has the capability to invade the privacy of every human being on Earth. Snowden stated that he had 'only disclosed information that is in the public's interest for now as the other documents are far too sensitive to release at this time for fear of causing harm to the human race'.

Around the time that President Obama gave a speech calling Snowden 'the most wanted man in the world' and a 'traitor to his country', Iran's largest independent news agency, Fars, ran a front page story claiming that Edward Snowden had documented proof that an 'alien intelligence agenda' is driving the US domestic and international policy. The Fars News Agency (deemed not just 'independent' but 'semi-official' by Reuters) claimed that the source of this information was the Russian FSB (KGB). Interestingly, Snowden is currently thought to be under President Putin's protection in Russia.

We are all familiar with persistent stories of UFO sightings (many cases have been witnessed by hundreds of people at a time, when passing above towns and cities). This is often explained away as military craft or space ships making trips into space. Now, there are large organisations in the world that would have us believe that humans can simply step into a commercially operated rocket/ship and visit the moon or orbit the Earth with nothing more than man-made technology.

There is, however, a growing minority who believe that the anti-matter propulsion systems required to venture into space was developed by the US Military with extra-terrestrial guidance. I probably don't have to remind you all about a recent failed private space venture costing billions of dollars, which resulted in a massive crash and a pilot fatality. The crash is said to have set the company back by one year, but personally I will be surprised if they ever reach their goal of making it into space successfully.

I conclude my endnote with a hope, dear reader. My hope is that the story will open your eyes to the bigger picture because I believe that we should be properly informed about what is going on now, on our beautiful planet.

Tallwhites.org